NO CLUE

NO CLUE

JAMES HAY

WILDSIDE PRESS

Originally published in 1919.

Published by Wildside Press LLC.
www.wildsidebooks.com

I

The Grey Envelope

Catherine Brace walked slowly from the mantel-piece to the open window and back again. Within the last hour she had done that many times, always to halt before the mantel and gaze at the oblong, grey envelope that leaned against the clock. Evidently, she regarded it as a powerful agency. An observer would have perceived that she saw tremendous things come out of it—and that she considered them with mingled satisfaction and defiance.

Her attitude, however, betrayed no hint of hesitation. Rather, the fixity of her gaze and the intensity of her mental concentration threw into high relief the hardness of her personality. She was singularly devoid of that quality which is generally called feminine softness.

And she was a forceful woman. She had power. It was in her lean, high-shouldered, ungraceful figure. It was in her thin, mobile lips and her high-bridged nose with its thin, clean-cut nostrils. She impressed herself upon her environment. Standing there at the mantel, her hands clasped behind her, she was so caught up by the possibilities of the future that she succeeded in imparting to the grey envelope an almost animate quality.

She became aware once more of voices in the next room: a man's light baritone in protest, followed by the taunt of her daughter's laugh. Although she left the mantel with lithe, swift step, it was with unusual deliberation that she opened the communicating door.

Her voice was free of excitement when, ignoring her daughter's caller, she said:

"Mildred, just a moment, please."

Mildred came in and closed the door. Her mother, now near the window across the room, looked first at her and then at the grey envelope.

"I thought," Mrs. Brace said, "you'd forgotten you were going to mail it."

"Why didn't you mail it yourself?" The tone of that was cool insolence.

Mother and daughter were strikingly alike—hair piled high in a wide wave above the forehead; black eyes too restless, but of that gleaming brilliance which heralds a refusal to grow old. So far, however, the daughter's features had not assumed an aspect of sharpness, like the mother's. One would have appraised the older woman vindictive—malevolent, possibly.

But in the younger face the mouth greatly softened, almost concealed, this effect of calculating hardness. Mildred Brace's lips had a softness of line, a vividness of colouring that indicated emotional depths utterly foreign to her mother.

They bore themselves now as if they commented on a decision already reached, a momentous step to which they had given immense consideration.

"I didn't mail it," Mrs. Brace answered her daughter's query, "because I knew, if you mailed it, you'd do as you'd said you wanted to do."

There was frank emphasis on the "said."

"Your feet don't always follow your intelligence, you know."

"I've been thinking about the thing," Mildred retorted, looking over her mother's shoulder into the summer night. "What's the use?"

"What's the use!" Mrs. Brace echoed, incredulous.

"Just that."

"We've been all over it! You know what it means to you—to both of us."

They spoke in low tones, careful that the man in the living room should not hear.

"My dear mother," Mildred said, with a return of her cool insolence, "you display a confidence hardly warranted by your—and our—man-experience."

She yawned slightly.

There was a harsher note in her mother's reply.

"He can't refuse. He can't!"

Mildred stared at the grey envelope a full three minutes. Mrs. Brace, wordless, showing no uneasiness as to the outcome, waited for her to speak.

"It's no use, mother," she said at last. "We can't manage it—him—this thing. It's too late."

The flat finality, the dreariness, of that announcement angered the older woman. Calmness fell from her. She came away from the window slowly, her hands clasped tightly at her back, the upper part of her body bending forward a little, her thin nostrils expanding and contracting to the force of her hurried breathing like leaves shaken in the wind. The curl of her thin lips added a curious ferocity to the words that passed them. She spoke, only when her face was within a few inches of Mildred's.

"No use!" she said contemptuously, her lowered voice explosive with passion. "Why? And why too late? Have you no self-respect, no will, no firmness? Are you all jelly and—"

She got hold of herself with remarkable effectiveness, throwing off the signs of her wrath as suddenly as they had appeared. She retreated a step and laughed, without mirth.

"Oh, well," she said, "it's your party, not mine, after all. But, in future, my dear, don't waste your time and mine in school-girl heroics."

She completed her retreat and stood again at the window. Her self-restraint was, in a way, fiercer than her rage—and it affected her daughter.

"You see," she concluded, "why I didn't mail it. I knew you wouldn't do the very thing you'd outlined."

Mildred looked at the envelope again. The pause that followed was broken by the man in the other room.

"Mildred," he called.

Mrs. Brace laughed silently. Mildred, seeing that ridicule, recoiled.

"What are you laughing at?" she demanded.

Her mother pointed to the communicating door.

"I was thinking of *that*," she said, "for life—and," she looked toward the grey envelope, "the other thing."

"I don't see—" Mildred began, and checked herself, gazing again at the envelope.

Her mother turned swiftly and stood looking into the night. The man called again and was not answered. The two women were motionless. There was no sound in the room, save the ticking of the clock on the mantel. Two minutes passed—three.

Mildred went toward the mantel, put out her hand, withdrew it. She became conscious of the excessive heat and touched her forehead with her handkerchief. She glanced at her mother's motionless figure, started to speak, closed her parted lips. Indecision shook her. She put out her hand again, picked up the envelope and stood tapping it against her left palm.

Mrs. Brace, without moving, spoke at last:

"It's a few minutes of twelve. If you catch the midnight collection, he'll get it, out there, by five o'clock tomorrow afternoon."

There was another pause.

Mildred went slowly to the door leading into the living room, and once more she was on the point of speaking.

Mrs. Brace was drumming her fingers on the window ledge. The action announced plainly that she had finished with the situation. Mildred put her hand on the knob, pulled the door half-open, closed it again.

"I've changed my mind," she said, dreariness still in her voice. "He can't refuse."

Her mother made no comment.

Mildred went into the living room.

"Gene," she said, with that indifference of tone which a woman employs toward a man she despises, "I'm going down to mail this."

"Well, I'll swear!" he quarreled sullenly. "Been in there all this time writing to him!"

"Yes! Look at it!" she taunted viciously, and waved the envelope before his eyes. "Sloanehurst!"

Taking up his hat, he went with her to the elevator.

II

The Woman on the Lawn

Mr. Jefferson Hastings, unsuspecting that he was about to be confronted with the most brutal crime in all his experience, regretted having come to "Sloanehurst." He disapproved of himself unreservedly. Clad in an ample, antique night-shirt, he stood at a window of the guest-room assigned to him and gazed over the steel rims of his spectacles into the hot, rainy night. His real vision, however, made no attempt to pierce the outer darkness. His eyes were turned inward, upon himself, in derision of his behaviour during the past three hours.

A kindly, reticent gentleman, who looked much older than his fifty-three years, he made it his habit to listen rather than talk. His wide fame as a criminologist and consulting detective had implanted no egotism in him. He abhorred the spotlight.

But tonight Judge Wilton, by skilful use of query, suggestion and reminder, had tempted him into talking "shop." He had been lured into the rôle of monologuist for the benefit of his host, Arthur Sloane. He had talked brilliantly, at length, in detail, holding his three hearers in spellbound and fascinated interest while he discoursed on crimes which he had probed and criminals whom he had known.

Not that he *thought* he had talked brilliantly! By no means! He was convinced that nine-tenths of the interest manifested in his remarks had been dictated by politeness. Old Hastings was just that sort of person; he discounted himself. He was in earnest, therefore, in his present self-denunciation. He sighed, remembering the volume of his discourse, the awful length of time in which he had monopolized the conversation.

But his modesty was not his only admirable characteristic. He had, also, a dependable sense of humour. It came to his relief now—he thought of his host, a chuckle throttling the beginnings of a second sigh deep down in his throat.

This was not the first time that Arthur Broughton Sloane had provoked a chuckle, although, for him, life was a house of terror, a torture chamber constructed with fiendish ingenuity. Mr. Sloane suffered from "nerves." He was spending his declining years in the arduous but surprisingly successful task of being wretched, irritable and ill-at-ease.

The variety of his agonies was equalled only by the alacrity with which he tested every cure or remedy of which he happened to hear. He agreed enthusiastically with his expensive physicians that he was neurasthenic, psychasthenic and neurotic.

His eyes were weak; his voice was weak; his spirit was weak. He shivered all day with terror at the idea of not sleeping at night. Every evening he quivered with horror at the thought of not waking up next morning. And yet, despite these absorbing, although not entirely delightful, preoccupations, Mr. Sloane was not without an object in life.

In fact, he had two objects in life: the happiness of his daughter, Lucille, and the study of crime and criminals. The latter interest had brought Hastings to the Sloane country home in Virginia. Judge Wilton, an old friend of the wrecked and wealthy Mr. Sloane, had met the detective on the street in Washington and urged:

"Go down to Sloanehurst and spend Saturday night. I'll be there when you arrive. Sloane's got his mind set on seeing you; and you won't regret it. His library on criminology will be a revelation, even to you."

And Hastings, largely because he shrank from seeming ungracious, had accepted Mr. Sloane's subsequent invitation.

Climbing now into the old-fashioned four-poster bed, he thought again of his conversation-spree and longed for self-justification. He sat up, sheetless, reflecting:

"As a week-ender, I'm a fine old chatter-box!—But young Webster got me! What did he say?—'The cleverer the criminal, the easier to run him down. The thug, acting on the spur of the moment, with a blow in the dark and a getaway through the night, leaves no trace behind him. Your "smart criminal" always overreaches himself.'—A pretty theory, but wild. Anyway, it made me forget myself; I talked my old fool head off."

He felt himself blush.

"Wish I'd let Wilton do the disproving; he was anxious enough."

A mental picture of Sloane consoled him once more.

"Silk socks and gingham gumption!" he thought. "But he's honest in his talk about being interested in crime. The man loves crime!—Good thing he's got plenty of money."

He fell asleep, in a kind of ruminative growl:

"Made a fool of myself—babbling about what *I* remembered—what *I* thought! I'll go back to Washington—in the morning."

Judge Wilton's unsteady voice, supplemented by a rattling of the doorknob, roused him. He had thrust one foot out of bed when Wilton came into the room.

"Quick! Come on, man!" the judge instructed, and hurried into the hall.

"What's wrong?" Hastings demanded, reaching for his spectacles.

Wilton, on his way down the stairs, flung back:

"A woman hurt—outside."

From the hall below came Mr. Sloane's high-pitched, complaining tones:

"Unfathomable angels! What do you say?—Who?"

Drawing on shoes and trousers, the detective overtook his host on the front verandah and followed him down the steps and around the northeast corner of the house. He noticed that Sloane carried in one hand an electric torch and in the other a bottle of smelling salts. It was no longer raining.

Rounding the corner, they saw, scarcely fifteen yards from the bay-window of the ballroom, the upturned face of a woman who lay prostrate on the lawn. Lights had been turned on in the house, making a glow which cut through the starless night.

The woman did not move. Judge Wilton was in the act of kneeling beside her.

"Hold on!" Hastings called out. "Don't disturb her—if she's dead."

"She is dead!" said Wilton.

"Who is she?" The detective, trying to find signs of life, put his hand over her heart.

"I don't know," Wilton answered the question. "Do you, Sloane?"

"Of course, I don't!"

Hastings said afterwards that Sloane's reply expressed astonished resentment that he should be suspected of knowing anybody vulgar enough to be murdered on his lawn.

The detective drew back his hand. His fingers were dark with blood.

At that moment Berne Webster, Lucille Sloane's fiancé, came from the rear of the house, announcing breathlessly:

"No phone connection—this time of night, judge.—It's past midnight.—I sent chauffeur—Lally—for the sheriff."

Hastings stood up, his first, cursory examination concluded.

"No doubt about it," he said. "She's dead.—Bring a blanket, somebody!"

Mr. Sloane's nerves had the best of him by this time. He trembled like a man with a chill, rattling the bottle of smelling salts against the metal end of his electric torch. He had on slippers and a light dressing gown over his pajamas.

Wilton was fully dressed, young Webster collarless but wearing a black, light-weight lounging jacket. Hastings was struck with the different degrees of their dress, or undress.

"Who found her?" he asked, looking at Webster.

"Judge Wilton—and I," said Webster, so short of breath that his chest heaved.

"How long ago?"

Wilton answered that:

"A few minutes, hardly five minutes. I ran in to call you and Sloane."

"And Mr.—you, Mr. Webster?"

"The judge told me to—to get the sheriff—by telephone."

Hastings knelt again over the woman's body.

"Here, Mr. Sloane," he ordered, "hold that torch closer, will you?"

Mr. Sloane found compliance impossible. He could not steady his hand sufficiently.

"Hold that torch, judge," Hastings prompted.

"It's knocked me out—completely," Sloane said, surrendering the torch to Wilton.

Webster, the pallor still on his face, a look of horror in his eyes, stood on the side of the body opposite the detective. At brief intervals he raised first one foot, then the other, clear of the ground and set it down again. He was unconscious of making any movement at all.

Hastings, thoroughly absorbed in the work before him, went about it swiftly, with now and then brief, murmured comment on what he did and saw. Although his ample night-shirt, stuffed into his equally baggy trousers, contributed nothing but comicality to his appearance, the others submitted without question to his domination. There was about him suddenly an atmosphere of power that impressed even the little group of awe-struck servants who stood a few feet away.

"Stabbed," he said, after he had run his hands over the woman's figure; "died instantly—must have. Got her heart.—Young—not over twenty-five, would you say?—Not dead long.—Anybody call a doctor?"

"I told Lally to stop by Dr. Garnet's house and send him—at once," Webster said, his voice low, and broken. "He's the coroner, too."

Hastings continued his examination. The brief pause that ensued was broken by a woman's voice:

"Pauline! Pauline!"

The call came from one of the upstairs windows. Hearing it, a woman in the servant group hurried into the house.

Webster groaned: "My God!"

"Frantic fiends! It gets worse and worse!" Sloane objected shrilly. "My nerves! And Lucille's annoyed—shocked!"

He held the smelling bottle to his nose, breathing deeply.

"Here! Take this!" Hastings directed, and put up his hand abruptly.

Sloane had so gone to pieces that the movement frightened him. He stepped back in such obvious terror that a hoarse guffaw of involuntary ridicule escaped one of the servants. The detective, finding that his kneeling posture made it difficult to put his handkerchief back into his trousers pocket, had thrust it toward Sloane. That gentleman having so suddenly removed himself out of reach, Hastings stuck the handkerchief into Judge Wilton's coat-pocket.

Arthur Sloane, the detective said later, never forgave him that unexpected wave of the handkerchief—and the servant's ridiculing laugh.

Hastings looked up to Wilton.

"Did you find any weapon?"

"I didn't look—didn't take time."

"Neither did I," young Webster added.

Hastings, disregarding the wet grass, was on his hands and knees, searching. He accomplished a complete circuit of the body, his round-shouldered, stooping figure making grotesque, elephantine shadows under the light of the torch as he moved about slowly, not trusting his eyes, but feeling with his hands every inch of the smallest, half-lit spaces.

Nobody else took part in the search. Having accepted his leadership from the outset, they seemed to take it for granted that he needed no help. Mentally benumbed by the horror of the tragedy, they stood there in the quiet, summer night, barren of ideas. They were like children, waiting to be instructed.

Hastings stood erect, pulling and hauling at his trousers.

"Can't find a knife or anything," he said. "Glad I can't. Hope he took it with him."

"Why?" asked Sloane, through chattering teeth.

"May help us to find him—may be a clue in the end."

He was silent a moment, squinting under the rims of his spectacles, looking down at the figure of the dead woman. He had already covered the face with the hat she had worn, a black straw sailor; but neither he nor the others found it easy to forget the peculiar and forbidding expression the features wore, even in death. It was partly fear, partly defiance—as if her last conscious thought had been a flitting look into the future, an exulting recognition of the certain consequences of the blow that had struck her down.

Put into words, it might have been: "You've murdered me, but you'll pay for it—terribly!"

A servant handed Hastings the blanket he had ordered. He looked toward the sky.

"I don't think it will rain any more," he said. "And it's best to leave things as they are until the coroner arrives.—He'll be here soon?"

"Should get here in half an hour or so," Judge Wilton informed him.

The detective arranged the blanket so that it covered the prone form completely, leaving the hat over the face as he had first placed it. With the exception of the hat, he had disturbed no part of the apparel. Even the folds of the raincoat, which fell away from the body and showed the rain-soaked black skirt, he left as he had found them. The white shirtwaist, also partly exposed now, was dry.

"Anybody move her hat before I came out?" he asked; "you, judge; or you, Mr. Webster?"

They had not touched it, they said; it was on the grass, beside her head, when they discovered the body, and they had left it there.

Again he was silent, brows drawn together as he stood over the murdered woman. Finally, he raised his head swiftly and, taking each in turn, searched sharply the countenances of the three men before him.

"Does—didn't anybody here know this woman?" he asked.

Berne Webster left his place at the opposite side of the body and came close to Hastings.

"I know who she is," he said, his voice lower even than before, as if he wished to keep that information from the servants.

Hastings' keen scrutiny had in it no intimation of surprise. Waiting for Webster to continue, he was addressed by the shivering Mr. Sloane:

"Mr. Hast—Mr. Hastings, take charge of—of things. Will you? You know about these things."

The detective accepted the suggestion.

"Suppose we get at what we know about it—what we all know. Let's go inside." He turned to the servants: "Stay here until you're called. See that nothing is disturbed, nothing touched."

He led the way into the house. Sloane, near collapse, clung to one of Judge Wilton's broad shoulders. It was young Webster who, as the little procession passed the hatrack in the front hall, caught up a raincoat and threw it over the half-clad Hastings.

III

The Unexpected Witness

In the library Hastings turned first to Judge Wilton for a description of the discovery of the body. The judge was in better condition than the others for connected narrative, Arthur Sloane had sunk into a morris chair, where he sighed audibly and plied himself by fits and starts with the aroma from the bottle of smelling salts. Young Webster, still breathing as if he had been through exhausting physical endeavour, stood near the table in the centre of the room, mechanically shifting his weight from foot to foot.

Wilton, seated half-across the room from Hastings, drew, absently, on a dead cigar-stump. A certain rasping note in his voice was his only remaining symptom of shock. He had the stern calmness of expression that is often seen in the broad, irregularly-featured face in early middle age.

"I can tell you in very few words," he said, addressing the detective directly. "We all left this room, you'll remember, at eleven o'clock. I found my bedroom uncomfortable, too warm. Besides, it had stopped raining. When I noticed that, I decided to go out and smoke my good-night cigar. This is what's left of it."

He put a finger to the unlighted stump still between his lips.

"What time did you go out?" asked Hastings.

"Probably, a quarter of an hour after I'd gone upstairs—fifteen or twenty minutes past eleven, I should guess."

"How did you go out—by what door?"

"The front door. I left it unlocked, but not open. At first I paced up and down, on the south side of the house, under the trees. It was reasonably light there then—that is to say, the clouds had thinned a little, and, after my eyes had got accustomed to it, I had no trouble in avoiding the trees and shrubbery.

"Then a cloud heavier than the others came up, I suppose. Anyway, it was much darker. There wasn't a light in the house, except in my room and Berne Webster's. Yours was out, I remember. I passed by the front of the house then, and went around to the north side. It was darker there, I thought, than it had been under the trees on the south side."

"How long had you been out then, altogether?"

"Thirty or forty minutes." He looked at his watch. "It's a quarter past twelve now. Let me see. I found the body a few minutes after I changed over to the north side. I guess I found it about five minutes before midnight—certainly not more than twenty minutes ago."

Hastings betrayed his impatience only by squinting under his spectacles and down the line of his nose, eying Wilton closely.

"All right, judge! Let's have it."

"I was going along slowly, very slowly, not doing much more than feeling my way with my feet on the close-shaven grass. It was the darkest night I ever saw. Literally, I couldn't have seen my hand in front of me.

"I had decided to turn about and go indoors when I was conscious of some movement, or slight sound, directly in front of me, and downward, at my feet. I got that impression."

"What movement? You mean the sound of a fall?"

"No; not that exactly."

"A footstep?"

"No. I hadn't any definite idea what sort of noise it was. I did think that, perhaps, it was a dog or a cat. Just then my foot came in contact with something soft. I stooped down instinctively, immediately.

"At that moment, that very second, a light flashed on in Arthur's bedroom. That's between this room and the big ballroom—on this floor, of course. That light threw a long, illuminating shaft into the murky darkness, the end of it coming just far enough to touch me and—what I found—the woman's body. I saw it by that light before I had time to touch it with my hand."

The judge stopped and drew heavily on his dead cigar.

"All right. See anything else?" Hastings urged.

"Yes; I saw Berne Webster. He had made the noise which attracted my attention."

"How do you know that?"

"He must have. He was stooping down, too, on the other side of the body, facing me, when the light went on—"

Sloane, twisting nervously in his chair, cut into Wilton's narrative.

"I can put this much straight," he said in shrill complaint: "I turned on the light you're talking about. I hadn't been able to sleep."

"Let's have this, one at a time, if you don't mind, Mr. Sloane," the detective suggested, watching Webster.

The young man, staring with fascinated intensity at Judge Wilton, seemed to experience some new horror as he listened.

"He was on the other side of it," the judge continued, "and practically in the same position that I was. We faced each other across the body. I think that describes the discovery, as you call it. We immediately examined the woman, looking for the wound, and found it. When we saw she was dead, we came in to wake you—and try to get a doctor. I told Berne to do that."

During the last few sentences Hastings had been walking slowly from his chair to the library door and back, his hands gouged deep into his trouser-pockets, folds of his night-shirt protruding from and falling over the waistband of the trousers, the raincoat hanging baggily from his shoulders. Ludicrous as the costume was, however, the old man so dominated them still that none of them, not even Wilton, questioned his authority.

And yet, the thing he was doing should have appealed to them as noteworthy. A man of less power could not have accomplished it. Coming from a sound sleep to the scene of a murder, he had literally picked up these men who had discovered it and who must be closely touched by it, had overcome their agitation, had herded them into the house and, with amazing promptness, had set about the task of getting from them the stories of what they knew and what they had done.

Appreciating his opportunity, he had determined to bring to light at once everything they knew. He devoted sudden attention now to Webster, whom he knew by reputation—a lawyer thirty years of age, brilliant in the criminal courts, and at present striving for a foothold in the more remunerative ranks of civil practice. He had never been introduced to him, however, before meeting him at Sloanehurst.

"Who touched that body first—Mr. Webster?" he demanded, his slow promenade uninterrupted as he kept his eyes on the lawyer's.

"Judge—I don't know, I believe," Webster replied uncertainly. "Who did, judge?"

"I want your recollection," Hastings insisted, kindly in spite of the unmistakable command of his tone. "That's why I asked you."

"Why?"

"For one thing, it might go far toward showing who was really first on the scene."

"I see; but I really don't remember. I'm not sure that either of us touched the body—just then. I think we both drew back, instinctively, when the light flashed on. Afterwards, of course, we both touched her—looking for signs of life."

The detective came to a standstill in front of Webster.

"Who reached the body first? Can you say?"

"No. I don't think either was first. We got there together."

"Simultaneously?"

"Yes."

"But I'm overlooking something. How did you happen to be there?"

"That's simple enough," Webster said, his brows drawn together, his eyes toward the floor, evidently making great effort to omit no detail of what had occurred. "I went to my room when we broke up here, at eleven. I read for a while. I got tired of that—it was close and hot. Besides, I never go to bed before one in the morning—that is, practically never. And I wasn't sleepy.

"I looked at my watch. It was a quarter to twelve. Like the judge, I noticed that it had stopped raining. I thought I'd have a better night's sleep if I got out and cooled off thoroughly. My room, the one I have this time, is close to the back stairway. I went down that, and out the door on the north side."

"Were you smoking?" Hastings put the query sharply, as if to test the narrator's nerves.

Webster's frown deepened.

"No. But I had cigarettes and matches with me. I intended to smoke—and walk about."

"But what happened?"

"It was so much darker than I had thought that I groped along with my feet, much as Judge Wilton did. I was making my way toward the front verandah. I went on, sliding my feet on the wet grass."

"Any reason for doing that, do you remember? Are there any obstructions there, anything but smooth, open lawn?"

"No. It was merely an instinctive act—in pitch dark, you know."

Webster, his eyes still toward the floor, waited for another question. Not getting it, he resumed:

"My foot struck something soft. I thought it was a wet cloak, something of that sort, left out in the rain. I hadn't heard a thing. And I had no premonition of anything wrong. I bent over, with nothing more than sheer idle curiosity, to put my hand on whatever the thing was. And just then the light went on in Mr. Sloane's bedroom. The judge and I were looking at each other across somebody lying on the ground, face upward."

"Either of you cry out?"

"No."

"Say anything?"

"Not much."

"Well, what?"

"I remember the judge said, 'Is she dead?' I said, 'How is she hurt?' We didn't say much while we were looking for the wound."

"Did you tell Judge Wilton you knew her?"

"No. There wasn't time for any explanation—specially."

"But you do know her?"

"I told you that, sir, outside—just now."

"All right. Who is she?" Hastings put that query carelessly, in a way which might have meant that he had heard the most important part of the young lawyer's story. That impression was heightened by his beginning again to pace the floor.

"Her name's Mildred Brace," replied Webster, moistening his lips with his tongue. "She was my stenographer for eight months."

The detective drew up sharply.

"When?"

"Until two weeks ago."

"She resign?"

"Yes. No—I discharged her."

"What for?"

"Incompetence."

"I don't understand that exactly. You mean you employed her eight months although she was incompetent?"

"That's pretty bald," Webster objected. "Her incompetence came, rather, from temperament. She was, toward the last, too nervous, excitable. She was more trouble than she was worth."

"Ah, that's different," Hastings said, with a significance that was clear. "People might have thought," he elaborated, "if you had fired her for other reasons, this tragedy tonight would have put you in an unenviable position—to say the least."

He had given words to the vague feeling which had depressed them all, ever since the discovery of the murder; that here was something vastly greater than the accidental finding of a person killed by an outsider, that the crime touched Sloanehurst personally. The foreboding had been patent—almost, it seemed, a tangible thing—but, until this moment, each had steered clear of it, in speech.

Webster's response was bitter.

"They'll want to say it anyway, I guess." To that he added, in frank resentment: "And I might as well enter a denial here: I had nothing to do with the—this whole lamentable affair!"

The silence in which he and Hastings regarded each other was broken by Arthur Sloane's querulous words:

"Why—why, in the name of all the inscrutable saints, this thing should have happened at Sloanehurst, is more than I can say! Jumping angels! Now, let me tell you what I—"

He stopped, hearing light footfalls coming down the hall. There was the swish of silk, a little outcry half-repressed, and Lucille Sloane stood in the doorway. One hand was at her breast, the other against the door-frame, to steady her tall, slightly swaying figure. Her hair, a pyramid on her head, as if the black, heavy masses of it had been done by hurrying fingers, gave to her unusual beauty now an added suggestion of dignity.

Profoundly moved as she was, there was nothing of the distracted or the inadequate about her. Hastings, who had admired her earlier in the evening, saw that her poise was far from overthrown. It seemed to him that she even had considered how to wear with extraordinary effect the brilliant, vari-coloured kimono draped about her. The only criticism of her possible was that, perhaps, she seemed a trifle too imperious—but, for his part, he liked that.

"A thoroughbred!" he catalogued her, mentally.

"You will excuse me, father," she said from the doorway, "but I couldn't help hearing." She thrust forward her chin. "Oh, I had to hear!— And there's something I have to tell."

Her glance went at last from Sloane to Hastings as she advanced slowly into the room.

The detective pushed forward a chair for her.

"That's fine, Miss Sloane," he assured her. "I'm sure you're going to help us."

"It isn't much," she qualified, "but I think it's important."

Still she looked at neither Berne Webster nor Judge Wilton. And only a man trained as Hastings was to keenness of observation would have seen the slight but incessant tremour of her fingers and the constant, convulsive play of the muscles under the light covering of her black silk slippers.

Sloane, alone, had remained seated. She was looking up to Hastings, who stood several feet in front of Webster and the judge.

"I had gone to sleep," she said, her voice low, but musical and clear. "I waked up when I heard father moving about—his room is directly under mine; and, now that Aunt Lucy is away, I'm always more or less anxious about him. And I knew he had got quiet earlier, gone to sleep. It wasn't like him to be awake again so soon.

"I sprang out of bed, really very quickly. I listened for a few seconds, but there was no further sound in father's room. The night was unusually quiet. There wasn't a sound—at first. Then I heard something. It was like somebody running, running very fast, outside, on the grass."

She paused. Hastings was struck by her air of alertness, or of prepared waiting, of readiness for questions.

"Which way did the footsteps go?" he asked.

"From the house—down the slope, toward the little gate that opens on the road."

"Then what?"

"I wondered idly what it meant, but it made no serious impression on me. I listened again for sounds in father's room. There was none. Struck again by the heavy silence—it was almost oppressive, coming after the rain—I went to the window. I stood there, I don't know how long. I think I was day-dreaming, lazily running things over in my mind. I don't think it was very long.

"And then father turned on the light in his room." She made a quick gesture with her left hand, wonderfully expressive of shock. "I shall never forget that! The long, narrow panel of light reached out into the dark like an ugly, yellow arm—reached out just far enough to touch and lay hold of the picture there on the grass; a woman lying on the drenched ground, her face up, and bending over her Judge Wilton and Berne—Mr. Webster.

"I knew she'd been hurt dreadfully; her feet were drawn up, her knees high; and I could see the looks of horror on the men's faces."

She paused, giving all her strength to the effort to retain her self-control before the assailing memory of what she had seen.

"That was all, Miss Sloane?" the detective prompted, in a kindly tone.

"Yes, quite," she said. "But I'd heard Berne's—what he was saying to you—and the judge's description of what they'd seen; and I thought you would like to know of the footsteps I'd heard—because they were the murderer's; they must have been. I knew it was important, most important."

"You were entirely right," he agreed warmly. "Thank you, very much."

He went the length of the room and halted by one of the bookcases, a weird, lumpy old figure among the shadows in the corner. He was scraping his cheek with his thumb, and looking at the ceiling, over the rims of his spectacles.

Arthur Sloane sighed his impatience.

"Those knees drawn up," Hastings said at last; "I was just thinking. They weren't drawn up when I saw the body. Were they?"

"We'd straightened the limbs," Webster answered. "Thought I'd mentioned that."

"No.—Then, there might have been a struggle? You think the woman had put up a fight—for her life?—and was overpowered?"

"Well," deliberated Webster, "perhaps; even probably."

"Strange," commented the detective, equally deliberate. "I hadn't thought so. I would have said she'd been struck down unawares—without the slightest warning."

IV

Hastings Is Retained

Arrival of the officials, Sheriff Crown and the coroner, Dr. Garnet, brought the conference to an abrupt close. Hastings, seeing the look in the girl's eyes, left the library in advance of the other men. Lucille followed him immediately.

"Mr. Hastings!"

"Yes, Miss Sloane?"

He turned and faced her.

"I must talk to you, alone. Won't you come in here?"

She preceded him into the parlour across the hall. When he put his hand on the electric switch, she objected, saying she preferred to be without the lights. He obeyed her. The glow from the hall was strong enough to show him the play of her features—which was what he wanted.

They sat facing each other, directly under the chandelier in the middle of the spacious room. He thought she had chosen that place to avoid all danger of being overheard in any direction. He saw, too, that she was hesitant, half-regretting having brought him there. He read her doubts, saw how pain and anxiety mingled in her wide-open grey eyes.

"Yes, I know," he said with a smile that was reassuring; "I don't look like a particularly helpful old party, do I?"

He liked her more and more. In presence of mind, he reflected, she surpassed the men of the household. In spite of the agitation that still kept her hands trembling and gave her that odd look of fighting desperately to hold herself together, she had formed a plan which she was on the point of disclosing to him.

Her courage impressed him tremendously. And, divining what her request would be, he made up his mind to help her.

"It's not that," she said, her lips twisting to the pretence of a smile. "I know your reputation—how brilliant you are. I was thinking you might not understand what I wanted to say."

"Try me," he encouraged. "I'm not that old!"

It occurred to him that she referred to Berne Webster and herself, fearing, perhaps, his lack of sympathy for a love affair.

"It's this," she began a rush of words, putting away all reluctance: "I think I realize more keenly than father how disagreeable this awful thing is going to be—the publicity, the newspapers, the questions, the photographs. I know, too, that Mr. Webster's in an unpleasant situation. I heard what he said to you in the library, every word of it.—But I don't have to think about him so much as about my father. He's a very sick man, Mr. Hastings. The shock of this, the resultant shocks lasting through days and weeks, may be fatal for him.

"Besides," she explained, attaining greater composure, "he is so nervous, so impatient of discomfort and irritating things, that he may bring upon himself the enmity of the authorities, the investigators. He may easily provoke them so that they would do anything to annoy him.

"I see you don't understand!" she lamented suddenly, turning her head away a little.

He could see how her lips trembled, as if she held them together only by immense resolution.

"I think I do," he contradicted kindly. "You want my help; isn't that it?"

"Yes." She looked at him again, with a quick turn of her head, her eyes less wide-open while she searched his face. "I want to employ you. Can't I—what do they call it?—retain you?"

"To do what, exactly?"

"Oh-h-h!" The exclamation had the hint of a sob in it; she was close to the end of her strength. "I'm a little uncertain about that. Can't you help me there? I want the real criminal found soon, immediately, as soon as possible. I want you to work on that. And, in the meantime, I want you to protect us—father—do things so that we shan't be overrun by reporters and detectives, all the dreadful results of the discovery of a murder at our very front door."

He was thoughtful, looking into her eyes.

"The fee is of no matter, the amount of it," she added impulsively.

"I wasn't thinking of that—although, of course, I don't despise fees. You see, the authorities, the sheriff, might not want my assistance, as you call it. Generally, they don't. They look upon it as interference and meddling."

"Still, you can work independently—retained by Mr. Arthur Sloane— can't you?"

He studied her further. For her age—hardly more than twenty-two— she was strikingly mature of face, and self-reliant. She had, he concluded, unusual strength of purpose; she was capable of large emotionalism, but mere feeling would never cloud her mind.

"Yes," he answered her; "I can do that. I will."

"Ah," she breathed, some of the tenseness going out of her, "you are very good!"

"And you will help me, of course."

"Of course."

"You can do so now," he pressed this point. "Why is it that all of you—I noticed it in the men in the library, and when we were outside, on the lawn—why is it that all of you think this crime is going to hit you, one of you, so hard? You seem to acknowledge in advance the guilt of one of you."

"Aren't you mistaken about that?"

"No. It struck me forcibly. Didn't you feel it? Don't you, now?"

"Why, no!"

He was certain that she was not frank with him.

"You mean," she added quickly, eyes narrowed, "I suspect—actually suspect some one in this house?"

In his turn, he was non-committal, retorting:

"Don't you?"

She resented his insistence.

"There is only one idea possible, I think," she declared, rising: "the footsteps that I heard fled from the house, not into it. The murderer is not here."

He stood up, holding her gaze.

"I'm your representative now, Miss Sloane," he said, his manner fatherly in its solicitude. "My duty is to save you, and yours, in every way I can—without breaking the law. You realize what my job is—do you?"

"Yes, Mr. Hastings."

"And the advisability, the necessity, of utter frankness between us?"

"Yes." She said that with obvious impatience.

"So," he persisted, "you understand my motive in asking you now: is there nothing more you can tell me—of what you heard and saw, when you were at your window?"

"Nothing—absolutely," she said, again obviously annoyed.

He was close to a refusal to have anything to do with the case. He was sure that she did not deal openly with him. He tried again:

"Nothing more, Miss Sloane? Think, please. Nothing to make you, us, more suspicious of Mr. Webster?"

"Suspect Berne!"

This time she was frank, he saw at once. The idea of the young lawyer's guilt struck her as out of the question. Her confidence in that was genuine, unalloyed. It was so emphatic that it surprised him. Why, then, this anxiety which had driven her to him for help? What caused the fear which, at the beginning of their interview, had been so apparent?

He thought with great rapidity, turning the thing over in his mind as he stood confronting her. If she did not suspect Webster, whom did she suspect? Her father?

That was it!—her father!

The discovery astounded Hastings—and appealed to his sympathy, tremendously.

"My poor child!" he said, on the warm impulse of his compassion.

She chose to disregard the tone he had used. She took a step toward the door, and paused, to see that he followed her.

He went nearer to her, to conclude what he had wanted to say:

"I shall rely on this agreement between us: I can come to you on any point that occurs to me? You will give me anything, and all the things, that may come to your knowledge as the investigation proceeds? Is it a bargain, Miss Sloane?"

"A bargain, Mr. Hastings," she assented. "I appreciate, as well as you do, the need of fair dealing between us. Anything else would be foolish."

"Fine! That's great, Miss Sloane!" He was still sorry for her. "Now, let me be sure, once for all: you're concealing nothing from me, no little thing even, on the theory that it would be of no use to me and, therefore, not worth discussing? You told us all you knew—in the library?"

She moved toward the door to the hall again.

"Yes, Mr. Hastings—and I'm at your service altogether."

He would have sworn that she was not telling the truth. This time, however, he had no thought of declining connection with the case. His compassion for her had grown.

Besides, her fear of her father's implication in the affair—was there foundation for it, more foundation than the hasty thought of a daughter still labouring under the effects of a great shock? He thought of Sloane, effeminate, shrill of voice, a trembling wreck, long ago a self-confessed ineffective in the battle of life—he, a murderer; he, capable of forceful action of any kind? It seemed impossible.

But the old man kept that idea to himself, and instructed Lucille.

"Then," he said, "you must leave things to me. Tell your father so. Tomorrow, for instance—rather this morning, for it's already a new day—reporters will come out here, and detectives, and the sheriff. All of them will want to question you, your father, all the members of the household. Refer them to me, if you care to.

"If you discuss theories and possibilities, you will only make trouble. To the sheriff, and anybody representing him, state the facts, the bare facts—that's all. May I count on you for that?"

"Certainly. That's why I've em—why I want your help: to avoid all the unpleasantness possible."

When she left him to go to her father's room, Hastings joined the group on the front verandah. Sheriff Crown and Dr. Garnet had already viewed the body.

"I'll hold the inquest at ten tomorrow morning, rather this morning," the coroner said. "That's hurrying things a little, but I'll have a jury here by then. They have to see the body before it's taken to Washington."

"Besides," observed the sheriff, "nearly all the necessary witnesses are here in this house party."

Aware of the Hastings fame, he drew the old man to one side.

"I'm going into Washington," he announced, "to see this Mrs. Brace, the girl's mother. Webster says she has a flat, up on Fourteenth street there. Good idea, ain't it?"

"Excellent," assured Hastings, and put in a suggestion: "You've heard of the fleeting footsteps Miss Sloane reported?"

"Yes. I thought Mrs. Brace might tell me who that could have been—some fellow jealous of the girl, I'll bet."

The sheriff, who was a tall, lanky man with a high, hooked nose and a pointed chin that looked like a large knuckle, had a habit of thrusting forward his upper lip to emphasize his words. He thrust it forward now, making his bristly, close-cropped red moustache stand out from his face like the quills of a porcupine.

"I'd thought of that—all that," he continued. "Looks like a simple case to me—very."

"It may be," said Hastings, sure now that Crown would not suggest their working together.

"Also," the sheriff told him, "I'll take this."

He held out the crude weapon with which, apparently, the murder had been committed. It was a dagger consisting of a sharpened nail file, about three inches long, driven into a roughly rounded piece of wood. This wooden handle was a little more than four inches in length and two inches thick. Hastings, giving it careful examination, commented:

"He shaped that handle with a pocket-knife. Then, he drove the butt-end of the nail file into it. Next, he sharpened the end of the file—put a razor edge on it.—Where did you get this, Mr. Crown?"

"A servant, one of the coloured women, picked it up as I came in. You were still in the library."

"Where was it?"

"About fifteen or twenty feet from the body. She stumbled on it, in the grass. Ugly thing, sure!"

"Yes," Hastings said, preoccupied, and added: "Let me have it again."

He took off his spectacles and, screwing into his right eye a jeweller's glass, studied it for several minutes. If he made an important discovery, he did not communicate it to Crown.

"It made an ugly hole," was all he said.

"You see the blood on it?" Crown prompted.

"Oh, yes; lucky the rain stopped when it did."

"When did it stop—out here?" Crown inquired.

"About eleven; a few minutes after I'd gone up to bed."

"So she was killed between eleven and midnight?"

"No doubt about that. Her hat had fallen from her head and was bottom up beside her. The inside of the crown and all the lower brim was dry as a bone, while the outside, even where it did not touch the wet grass, was wet. That showed there wasn't any rain after she was struck down."

The sheriff was impressed by the other's keenness of observation.

"That's so," he said. "I hadn't noticed it."

He sought the detective's opinion.

"Mr. Hastings, you've just heard the stories of everybody here. Do me a favour, will you? Is it worth while for me to go into Washington? Tell me: do you think anybody here at Sloanehurst is responsible for this murder?"

"Mr. Crown," the old man answered, "there's no proof that anybody here killed that woman."

"Just what I thought," Mr. Crown applauded himself. "Glad you agree with me. It'll turn out a simple case. Wish it wouldn't. Nominating primary's coming on in less than a month. I'd get a lot more votes if I ran down a mysterious fellow, solved a tough problem."

He strode down the porch steps and out to his car—for the ten-mile run into Washington. Hastings was strongly tempted to accompany him, even without being invited; it would mean much to be present when the mother first heard of her daughter's death.

But he had other and, he thought, more important work to do. Moving so quietly that his footsteps made no sound, he gained the staircase in the hall and made his way to the second floor. If anybody had seen him and inquired what he intended to do, he would have explained that he was on his way to get his own coat in place of the one which young Webster had, with striking thoughtfulness, thrown over him.

As a matter of fact, his real purpose was to search Webster's room.

But experience had long since imbued him with contempt for the obvious. Secure from interruption, since his fellow-guests were still in the library, he did not content himself with his hawk-like scrutiny of the one room; he explored the back stairway which had been Webster's exit to the lawn, Judge Wilton's room, and his own.

In the last stage of the search he encountered his greatest surprise. Looking under his own bed by the light of a pocket torch, he found that one of the six slats had been removed from its place and laid cross-ways upon the other five. The reason for this was apparent; it had been shortened by between four and five inches.

"Cut off with a pocket-knife," the old man mused; "crude work, like the shaping of the handle of that dagger—downstairs; same wood, too. And in my room, from my bed—

"I wonder—"

With a low whistle, expressive of incredulity, he put that new theory from him and went down to the library.

V

The Interview with Mrs. Brace

Gratified, and yet puzzled, by the results of his search of the upstairs rooms, Hastings was fully awake to the necessity of his interviewing Mrs. Brace as soon as possible. Lally, the chauffeur, drove him back to Washington early that Sunday morning. It was characteristic of the old man that, as they went down the driveway, he looked back at Sloanehurst and felt keenly the sufferings of the people under its roof.

He was particularly drawn to Lucille Sloane, with whom he had had a second brief conference. While waiting for his coffee—nobody in the house had felt like breakfast—he had taken a chair at the southeast end of the front porch and, pulling a piece of soft wood and a knife from his Gargantuan coat-pockets, had fallen to whittling and thinking.—Whittling, he often said, enabled him to think clearly; it was to him what tobacco was to other men.

Thus absorbed, he suddenly heard Lucille's voice, low and tense:

"We'll have to leave it as it was be—"

Berne Webster interrupted her, a grain of bitterness in his words:

"Rather an unusual request, don't you think?"

"I wanted to tell you this after the talk in the library," she continued, "but there—"

They had approached Hastings from the south side of the house and, hidden from him by the verandah railing, were upon him before he could make his presence known. Now, however, he did so, warning them by standing up with a clamorous scraping of his feet on the floor. Instinctively, he had recoiled from overhearing their discussion of what was, he thought, a love-affair topic.

Lucille hurried to him, not that she had additional information to give him, but to renew her courage. Having called upon him for aid, she had in the usual feminine way decided to make her reliance upon him complete. And, under the influence of his reassuring kindliness, her hesitance and misgivings disappeared.

He had judged her feelings correctly during their conference in the parlour. At dinner, she had seen in him merely a pleasant, quiet-spoken old man, a typical "hick" farmer, who wore baggy, absurdly large clothing—

"for the sake of his circulation," he said—and whose appearance in no way corresponded to his reputation as a learned psychologist and investigator of crime. Now, however, she responded warmly to his charm, felt the sincerity of his sympathy.

Seeing that she looked up to him, he enjoyed encouraging her, was bound more firmly to her interests.

"I think your fears are unfounded," he told her.

But he did not reveal his knowledge that she suspected her father of some connection with the murder. In fact, he could not decide what her suspicion was exactly, whether it was that he had been guilty of the crime or that he had guilty knowledge of it.

A little anxious, she had asked him to promise that he would be back by ten o'clock, for the inquest. He thought he could do that, although he had persuaded the coroner that his evidence would not be necessary—the judge and Webster had found the body; their stories would establish the essential facts.

"Why do you want me here then?" he asked, not comprehending her uneasiness.

"For one thing," she said, "I want you to talk to father—before the inquest. I wish you could now, but he isn't up."

It was eight o'clock when Miss Davis, telephone operator in the cheap apartment house on Fourteenth street known as The Walman, took the old man's card and read the inscription, over the wire:

"'Mr. Jefferson Hastings.'"

After a brief pause, she told him:

"She wants to know if you are a detective."

"Tell her I am."

"You may go up," the girl reported. "It's Number Forty-three, fourth floor—no elevator."

After ascending the three flights of stairs, he sat down on the top step, to get his breath. Mr. Hastings was stout, not to say sebaceous—and he proposed to begin the interview unhandicapped.

Mrs. Brace answered his ring. There was nobody else in the apartment. The moment he looked into her restless, remarkably brilliant black eyes, he catalogued her as cold and repellent.

"One of the swift-eyed kind," he thought; "heart as hard as her head. No blood in her—but smart. Smart!"

He relied, without question, on his ability to "size up" people at first glance. It was a gift with him, like the intuition of women; and to it, he thought, he owed his best work as a detective.

Mrs. Brace, without speaking, without acknowledging his quiet "Mrs. Brace, I believe?" led him into the living room after waiting for him to close the entrance door. This room was unusually large, out of proportion to the rest of the apartment which included, in addition to the narrow entry, a bedroom, kitchen and bath—all, so far as his observation went, sparsely and cheaply furnished.

They sat down, and still she did not speak, but studied his face. He got the impression that she considered all men her enemies and sought some intimation of what his hostility would be like.

"I'm sorry to trouble you at such a time," he began. "I shall be as brief as possible."

Her black eyebrows moved upward, in curious interrogation. They were almost mephistophelian, and unpleasantly noticeable, drawn thus nearer to the wide wave of her white hair.

"You wanted to see me—about my daughter?"

Her voice was harsh, metallic, free of emotion. There was nothing about her indicative of grief. She did not look as if she had been weeping. He could learn nothing from her manner; it was extremely matter-of-fact, and chilly. Only, in her eyes he saw suspicion—perhaps, he reflected, suspicion was always in her eyes.

Her composure amazed him.

"Yes," he replied gently; "if I don't distress you—"

"What is it?"

She suddenly lowered her eyebrows, drew them together until they were a straight line at the bottom of her forehead.

Her cold self-possession made it easy, in fact necessary, for him to deal with facts directly. Apparently, she resented his intimated condolence. He could fling any statement, however sensational, against the wall of her indifference. She was, he decided, as free of feeling as she was inscrutable. She would be surprised by emotion into nothing. It was his brain against hers.

"I want to say first," he continued, "that my only concern, outside of my natural and very real sympathy with such a loss as yours must be, is to find the man who killed her."

She moved slowly to and fro on the armless, low-backed rocker, watching him intently.

"Will you help me?"

"If I can."

"Thank you," he said, smiling encouragement from force of habit, not because he expected to arouse any spirit of cooperation in her. "I may ask you a few questions then?"

"Certainly."

Her thin nostrils dilated once, quickly, and somehow their motion suggested the beginning of a ridiculing smile. He went seriously to work.

"Have you any idea, Mrs. Brace, as to who killed your daughter—or could have wanted to kill her?"

"Yes."

"Who?"

She got up, without the least change of expression, without a word, and, as she crossed the room, paused at the little table against the farther wall to arrange more symmetrically a pile of finger-worn periodicals. She went through the communicating door into the bedroom, and, from where he sat, he could see her go through another door—into the bathroom, he guessed. In a moment, he heard a glass clink against a faucet. She had gone for a drink of water, to moisten her throat, like an orator preparing to deliver an address.

She came back, unhurried, imperturbable, and sat down again in the armless rocker before she answered his question. So far as her manner might indicate, there had been no interruption of the conversation.

He swept her with wondering eyes. She was not playing a part, not concealing sorrow. The straight, hard lines of her lean figure were a complement to her gleaming, unrevealing eyes. There was hardness about her, and in her, everywhere.

A slow, warm breeze brought through the curtainless window a disagreeable odour, sour and fetid. The apartment was at the back of the building; the odour came from a littered courtyard, a conglomeration of wet ashes, neglected garbage, little filthy pools, warmed into activity by the sun, high enough now to touch them. He could see the picture without looking—and that odour struck him as excruciatingly appropriate to this woman's soul.

"Berne Webster killed my daughter," she said evenly, hands moveless in her lap. "There are several reasons for my saying so. Mildred was his stenographer for eight months, and he fell in love with her—that was the way he described his feeling, and intention, toward her. The usual thing happened; he discharged her two weeks ago.

"He wants to marry money. You know about that, I take it—Miss Sloane, daughter of A. B. Sloane, Sloanehurst, where she was murdered. They're engaged. At least, that is—was Mildred's information, although the engagement hasn't been announced, formally. Fact is, he has to marry the Sloane girl."

Her thin, mobile lips curled upward at the ends and looked a little thicker, giving an exaggerated impression of wetness. Hastings thought of some small, feline animal, creeping, anticipating prey—a sort of calculating ferocity.

She talked like a person bent on making every statement perfectly clear and understandable. There was no intimation that she was so communicative because she thought she was obliged to talk. On the contrary, she welcomed the chance to give him the story.

"Have you told all this to that sheriff, Mr. Crown?" he inquired.

"Yes; but he seemed to attach no importance to it."

She coloured her words with feeling at last—it was contempt—putting the sheriff beyond the pale of further consideration.

"You were saying Mr. Webster had to marry Miss Sloane. What do you mean by that, Mrs. Brace?"

"Money reasons. He had to have money. His bank balance is never more than a thousand dollars. He's got to produce sixty-five thousand dollars by the seventh of next September. This is the sixteenth of July. Where is he to get all that? He's got to marry it."

Hastings put more intensity into his scrutiny of her smooth, untroubled face. It showed no sudden access of hatred, no unreasoning venom, except that the general cast of her features spoke generally of vindictiveness. She was, unmistakably, sure of what she said.

"How do you know that?" he asked, hiding his surprise.

"Mildred knew it—naturally, from working in his office."

"Let me be exact, Mrs. Brace. Your charge is just what?"

He felt the need of keen thought. He reached for his knife and piece of wood. Entirely unconsciously, he began to whittle, letting little shavings fall on the bare floor. She made no sign of seeing his new occupation.

"It's plain enough, Mr.—I don't recall your name."

"Hastings—Jefferson Hastings."

"It's plain and direct, Mr. Hastings. He threw her over, threw Mildred over. She refused to be dealt with in that way. He wouldn't listen to her side, her arguments, her protests, her pleas. She pursued him; and last night he killed her. I understand—Mr. Crown told me—he was found bending over the body—it seemed to me, caught in the very commission of the crime."

A fleeting contortion, like mirthless ridicule, touched her lips as she saw him, with head lowered, cut more savagely into the piece of wood. She noticed, and enjoyed, his dismay.

"That isn't quite accurate," he said, without lifting his head. "He and another man, Judge Wilton, stumbled—came upon your daughter's body at the same moment."

"Was that it?" she retorted, unbelieving.

When he looked up, she was regarding him thoughtfully, the black brows elevated, interrogative. The old man felt the stirrings of physical nausea within him. But he waited for her to elaborate her story.

"Do you care to ask anything more?" she inquired, impersonal as ashes.

"If I may."

"Why, certainly."

He paused in his whittling, brought forth a huge handkerchief, passed it across his forehead, was aware for a moment that he was working hard against the woman's unnatural calmness, and feeling the heat intensely. She was untouched by it. He whittled again, asking her:

"You a native of Washington?"

"No."

"How long have you been here?"

"About nine months. We came from Chicago."

"Any friends here—have you any friends here?"

"Neither here nor elsewhere." She made that bleak declaration simply, as if he had suggested her possession of green diamonds. Her tone made friendship a myth.

He felt again utterly free of the restraints and little hesitancies usual in situations of this nature.

"And your means, resources. Any, Mrs. Brace?"

"None—except my daughter's."

He was unaccountably restless. Putting the knife into his pocket, he stood up, went to the window. His guess had been correct. The courtyard below was as he had pictured it. He stood there at least a full minute.

Turning suddenly in the hope of catching some new expression on her face, he found her gazing steadily, as if in revery, at the opposite wall.

"One thing more, Mrs. Brace: did you know your daughter intended to go to Sloanehurst last night?"

"No."

"Were you uneasy when she failed to come in—last night?"

"Yes; but what could I do?"

"Had she written to Mr. Webster recently?"

"Yes; I think so."

"You think so?"

"Yes; she went out to mail a letter night before last. I recall that she said it was important, had to be in the box for the midnight collection, to reach its destination yesterday afternoon—late. I'm sure it was to Webster."

"Did you see the address on it?"

"I didn't try to."

He stepped from the window, to throw the full glare of the morning sky on her face, which was upturned, toward him.

"Was it in a grey envelope?"

"Yes; an oblong, grey envelope," she said, the impassive, unwrinkled face unmoved to either curiosity or reticence.

With surprising swiftness he took a triangular piece of paper from his breast pocket and held it before her.

"Might that be the flap of that grey envelope?"

She inspected it, while he kept hold of it.

"Very possibly."

Without leaving her chair, she turned and put back the lid of a rickety little desk in the corner immediately behind her. There, she showed him, was a bundle of grey envelopes, the corresponding paper beside it. He compared the envelope flaps with the one he had brought. They were identical.

Here was support of her assertion that Berne Webster had been pursued by her daughter as late as yesterday afternoon—and, therefore, might have been provoked into desperate action. He had found that scrap of grey paper at Sloanehurst, in Webster's room.

VI

Action by the Sheriff

Mrs. Brace did not ask Hastings where he had got the fragment of grey envelope. She made no comment whatever.

He reversed the flap in his hand and showed her the inner side on which were, at first sight, meaningless lines and little smears. He explained that the letter must have been put into the envelope when the ink was still un-dried on the part of it that came in contact with the flap, and, the paper being of that rough-finish, spongy kind frequently affected by women, the flap had absorbed the undried ink pressed against it.

"Have you a hand-mirror?" he asked, breaking a long pause.

She brought one from the bedroom. Holding it before the envelope flap, he showed her the marks thus made legible. They were, on the first line: "—edly de—," with the first loop or curve of an "n" or an "m" fol-lowing the "de"; and on the second line the one word "Pursuit!" the whole reproduction being this:

edly de
Pursuit!

"Does that writing mean anything to you, Mrs. Brace?" Hastings asked, keeping it in front of her.

She moved her left hand, a quiet gesture indicating her lack of further interest in the piece of paper.

"Nothing special," she said, "except that the top line seems to bear out what I've told you. It might be: 'repeatedly demanded'—I mean Mildred may have written that she had repeatedly demanded justice of him, some-thing of that sort."

"Is it your daughter's writing?"

"Yes."

"And the word 'Pursuit,' with an exclamation point after it? That sug-gest anything to you?"

"Why, no." She showed her first curiosity: "Where did you get that piece of envelope?"

"Not from Berne Webster," he said, smiling.

"I suppose not," she agreed, and did not press him for the information.

"You said," he went to another point, "that the sheriff attached no importance to your belief in Webster's guilt. Can you tell me why?"

Her contempt was frank enough now, and visible, her lips thickening and assuming the abnormally humid appearance he had noticed before.

"He thinks the footsteps which Miss Sloane says she heard are the deciding evidence. He accuses a young man named Russell, Eugene Russell, who's been attentive to Mildred."

Hastings was relieved.

"Crown's seen him, seen Russell?" he asked, not troubling to conceal his eagerness.

On that, he saw the beginnings of wrath in her eyes. The black eyebrows went upward, the thin nostrils expanded, the lips set to a line no thicker than the edge of a knife.

"You, too, will—"

She broke off, checked by the ringing of the wall telephone in the entrance hall. She answered the call, moving without haste. It was for Mr. Hastings, she said, going back to her seat.

He regretted the interruption; it would give her time to regain the self-control she had been on the point of losing.

Sheriff Crown was at the other end of the wire. He was back at Sloanehurst, he explained, and Miss Sloane had asked him to give the detective certain information:

He had asked the Washington police to hold Eugene Russell, or to persuade him to attend the inquest at Sloanehurst. Crown, going in to Washington, had stopped at the car barns of the electric road which passed Sloanehurst, and had found a conductor who had made the ten-thirty run last night. This conductor, Barton, had slept at the barns, waiting for the early-morning resumption of car service to take him to his home across the city.

Barton remembered having seen a man leave his car at Ridgecrest, the next stop before Sloanehurst, at twenty-five minutes past ten last night. He answered Russell's description, had seemed greatly agitated, and was unfamiliar with the stops on the line, having questioned Barton as to the distance between Ridgecrest and Sloanehurst. That was all the conductor had to tell.

"Mrs. Brace's description of Russell, a real estate salesman who had been attentive to her daughter," continued Crown, "tallied with Barton's description of the man who had been on his car. I got his address from her. But say! She don't fall for the idea that Russell's guilty! She gave me to understand, in that snaky, frozen way of hers, that I was a fool for thinking so.

"Anyway, I'm going to put him over the jumps!" The sheriff was highly elated. "What was he out here for last night if he wasn't jealous of the girl?

Wasn't he following her? And, when he came up with her on the Sloanehurst lawn, didn't he kill her? It looks plain to me; simple. I told you it was a simple case!"

"Have you seen him?" Hastings was looking at his watch as he spoke—it was nine o'clock.

"No; I went to his boarding house, waked up the place at three o'clock this morning. He wasn't there."

Hastings asked for the number of the house. It was on Eleventh street, Crown informed him, and gave the number.

"I searched his room," the sheriff added, his voice self-congratulatory.

"Find anything?"

"I should say! The nail file was missing from his dressing case."

"What else?"

"A pair of wet shoes—muddy and wet."

"Then, he'd returned to his room, after the murder, and gone out again?"

"That's it—right."

"Anybody in the house hear him come in, or go out?"

"Not a soul.—And I don't know where he is now."

Hastings, leaving the telephone, found Mrs. Brace carefully brushing into a newspaper the litter made by his whittling. Her performance of that trivial task, the calm thoroughness with which she went about it, or the littleness of it, when compared with her complete indifference to the tragedy which should have overwhelmed her—something, he could not tell exactly what, made her more repugnant to him than ever.

He spoke impulsively:

"Did you want—didn't you feel some impulse, some desire, to go out there when you heard of this murder?"

She paused in her brushing, looking up to him without lifting herself from hands and knees.

"Why should I have wanted to do any such thing?" she replied. "Mildred's not out there. What's out there is—nothing."

"Do you know about the arrangements for the removal of the body?"

"The sheriff told me," she replied, cold, impersonal. "It will be brought to an undertaking establishment as soon as the coroner's jury has viewed it."

"Yes—at ten o'clock this morning."

She made no comment on that. He had brought up the disagreeable topic—one which would have been heart-breaking to any other mother he had ever known—in the hope of arousing some real feeling in her. And he had failed. Her self-control was impregnable. There was about her an atmosphere that was, in a sense, terrifying, something out of all nature.

She brushed up the remaining chips and shavings while he got his hat.

He was deliberating: was there nothing more she could tell him? What could he hope to get from her except that which she wanted to tell? He was sure that she had spoken, in reply to each of his questions, according to a prearranged plan, a well designed scheme to bring into high relief anything that might incriminate Berne Webster.

And he was by no means in a mood to persuade himself of Webster's guilt. He knew the value of first impressions; and he did not propose to let her clog his thoughts with far-fetched deductions against the young lawyer.

She got to her feet with cat-like agility, and, to his astonishment, burst into violent speech:

"You're standing there trying to think up things to help Berne Webster! Like the sheriff! Now, I'll tell you what I told him: Webster's guilty. I know it! He killed my daughter. He's a liar and a coward—a traitor! He killed her!"

There was no doubt of her emotion now. She stood in a strange attitude, leaning a little toward him in the upper part of her body, as if all her strength were consciously directed into her shoulders and neck. She seemed larger in her arms and shoulders; they, with her head and face, were, he thought, the most vivid part of her—an effect which she produced deliberately, to impress him.

Her whole body was not tremulous, but, rather, vibrant, a taut mechanism played on by the rage that possessed her. Her eyebrows, high on her forehead, reminded him of things that crawled. Her eyes, brilliant like clear ice with sunshine on it, were darting, furtive, always in motion.

She did not look him squarely in the eye, but her eyes selected and bored into every part of his face; her glance played on his countenance. He could easily have imagined that it burned him physically in many places.

"All this talk about Gene Russell's being guilty is stuff, bosh!" she continued. "Gene wouldn't hurt anybody. He couldn't! Wait until you see him!" Her lips curled momentarily to their thickened, wet sneer. "There's nothing to him—nothing! Mildred hated him; he bored her to death. Even I laughed at him. And this sheriff talks about the boy's having killed her!"

Suddenly, she partially controlled her fury. He saw her eyes contract to the gleam of a new idea. She was silent a moment, while her vibrant, tense body swayed in front of him almost imperceptibly.

When she spoke again, it was in her flat, constrained tone. He was impressed anew with her capacity for making her feeling subordinate to her intelligence.

"She's a dangerous woman," he thought again.

"You're working for Webster?"

Her inquiry came after so slight a pause, and it was put to him in a manner so different from the unrestraint of her denunciation of Webster, that he felt as he would have done if he had been dealing with two women.

"I've told you already," he said, "my only interest is in finding the real murderer. In that sense, I'm working for Webster—if he's innocent."

"But he didn't hire you?"

"No."

Seeing that he told the truth, she indulged herself in rage again. It was just that, Hastings thought; she took an actual, keen pleasure in giving vent to the anger that was in her. Relieved of the necessity of censoring her words and thoughts closely, she could say what she wanted to say.

"He's guilty, and I'll prove it!" she defied the detective's disbelief. "I'll help to prove it. Guilty? I tell you he is—guilty as hell!"

He made an abrupt departure, her shrill hatred ringing in his ears when he reached the street. He found it hard, too, to get her out of his eyes, even now—she had impressed herself so shockingly upon him. The picture of her floated in front of him, above the shimmering pavement, as if he still confronted her in all her unloveliness, the smooth, white face like a travesty on youth, the swift, darting eyes, the hard, straight lines of the lean figure, the cold deliberation of manner and movement.

"She's incapable of grief!" he thought. "Terrible! She's terrible!"

Lally drove him to his apartment on Fifteenth street, where the largest of three rooms served him as a combination library and office. There he kept his records, in a huge, old-fashioned safe; and there, also, he held his conferences, from time to time, with police chiefs and detectives from all parts of the country when they sought his help in their pursuit of criminals.

The walls were lined with books from floor to ceiling. A large table in the centre of the room was stacked high with newspapers and magazines. Dusty papers and books were piled, too, on several chairs set against the bookcases, and on the floor in one corner was a pyramid of documents.

"This place is like me," he explained to visitors; "it's loosely dressed."

He sat down at the table and wrote instructions for one of his two assistants, his best man, Hendricks. Russell's room must be searched and Russell interviewed—work for which Hastings felt that he himself could not spare the time. He gave Hendricks a second task: investigation of the financial standing of two people: Berne Webster and Mrs. Catherine Brace.

He noted, with his customary kindness, in his memorandum to Hendricks:

"Sunday's a bad day for this sort of work, but do the best you can. Report tomorrow morning."

That arranged, he set out for Sloanehurst, to keep his promise to Lucille—he would be there for the inquest.

On the way he reviewed matters:

"Somehow, I got the idea that the Brace woman *knew* Russell hadn't killed her daughter. Funny, that is. How could she have known that? How can she know it now?

"She's got the pivotal fact in this case. I felt it. I'm willing to bet she persuaded her daughter to pursue Webster. And things have gone 'bust'—didn't come out as she thought they would. What was she after, money? That's exactly it! Exactly! Her daughter could hold up Webster, and Webster could hold up the Sloanes after his marriage."

He whistled softly.

"If she can prove that Webster should have married her daughter, that he's in need of anything like sixty-five thousand dollars—where does he get off? He gets off safely if the Brace woman ever sees fit to tell—what? I couldn't guess if my whittling hand depended on it." He grimaced his repugnance.

"What a woman! A mania for wickedness—evil from head to foot, thoroughly. *She* wouldn't stick at murder—if she thought it safe. She'd do anything, say anything. Every word she uttered this morning had been rehearsed in her mind—with gestures, even. When I beat her, I beat this puzzle; that's sure."

That he had to do with a puzzle, he had no manner of doubt. The very circumstances surrounding the discovery of the girl's body—Arthur Sloane flashing on the light in his room at a time when his being awake was so unusual that it frightened his daughter; Judge Wilton stumbling over the dead woman; young Webster doing the same thing in the same instant; the light reaching out to them at the moment when they bent down to touch the thing which their feet had encountered—all that shouted mystery to his experienced mind.

He thought of Webster's pronouncement: "The thug, acting on the spur of the moment, with a blow in the dark and a getaway through the night—" Here was reproduction of that in real life. Would people say that Webster had given himself away in advance? They might.

And the weapon, what about that? It could have been manufactured in ten minutes. Crown had said over the wire that Russell's nail file was missing. What if Webster's, too, were missing? He would see—although he expected to uncover no such thing.

He came, then, to Lucille's astounding idea, that her father must be "protected," because he was nervous and, being nervous, might incur the enmity of the authorities. He could not take that seriously. And yet the most fruitful imagination in the world could fabricate no motive for Arthur Sloane's killing a young woman he had never seen.

Only Webster and Russell could be saddled with motives: Webster's, desperation, the savage determination to rid himself of the woman's pursuit; Russell's, unreasoning jealousy.

So far as facts went, the crime lay between those two—and he could not shake off the impression that Mrs. Brace, shrilly asserting Russell's innocence, had known that she spoke the absolute truth.

VII

The Hostility of Mr. Sloane

Delayed by a punctured tire, Hastings reached Sloanehurst when the inquest was well under way. He went into the house by a side door and found Lucille Sloane waiting for him.

"Won't you go to father at once?" she urged him.

"What's the matter?" He saw that her anxiety had grown during his absence.

"He's in one of his awfully nervous states. I hope you'll be very patient with him—make allowances. He doesn't seem to grasp the importance of your connection with the case; wants to ask questions. Won't you let me take you to him, now?"

"Why, yes, if I can be of any help. What do you want me to say to him?"

As a matter of fact, he was glad of the opportunity for the interview. He had long since discovered the futility of inquests in the uncovering of important evidence, and he had not intended to sit through this one. He wanted particularly to talk to Berne Webster, but Sloane also had to be questioned.

"I thought you might explain," she continued hurriedly, preceding him down the hall toward her father's room, "that you will do exactly what I asked you to do—see that the mysterious part of this terrible affair, if there is any mystery in it—see that it's cleared up promptly. Please tell him you'll act for us in dealing with newspaper reporters; that you'll help us, not annoy us, not annoy him."

She had stopped at Sloane's door.

"And you?" Hastings delayed her knock. "If they want you to testify, if Dr. Garnet calls for you, I think you'd better testify very frankly, tell them about the footsteps you heard."

"I've already done that." She seemed embarrassed. "Father asked me to phone Mr. Southard, Mr. Jeremy Southard, his lawyer, about it. I know I told you I wanted your advice about everything. I would have waited to ask you. But you were late. I had to take Mr. Southard's advice."

"That's perfectly all right," he reassured her. "Mr. Southard advised you wisely.—Now, I'm going to ask your help. The guest-rooms upstairs—

have the servants straightened them up this morning?"

They had not, she told him. Excitement had quite destroyed their efficiency for the time being; they were at the parlour windows, listening, or waiting to be examined by the coroner.

"That's what I hoped," he said. "Won't you see that those rooms are left exactly as they are until I can have a look at them?" She nodded assent. "And say nothing about my speaking of it—absolutely nothing to anybody? It's vitally important."

The door was opened by Sloane's man, Jarvis, who had in queer combination, Hastings thought, the salient aspects of an undertaker and an experienced pick-pocket. He was dismal of countenance and alert in movement, an efficient ghost, admirably appropriate to the twilit gloom of the room with its heavily shaded windows.

Mr. Sloane was in bed, in the darkest corner.

"Father," Lucille addressed him from the door-sill, "I've asked Mr. Hastings to talk to you about things. He's just back from Washington."

"Shuddering saints!" said Mr. Sloane, not lifting his head from the pillows.

Lucille departed. The ghostly Jarvis closed the door without so much as a click of the latch. Hastings advanced slowly toward the bed, his eyes not yet accustomed to the darkness.

"Shuddering, shivering, shaking saints!" Mr. Sloane exclaimed again, the words coming in a slow, shrill tenor from his lips, as if with great exertion he reached up with something and pushed each one out of his mouth. "Sit down, Mr. Hastings, if I can control my nerves, and stand it. What is it?"

His hostility to the caller was obvious. The evident and grateful interest with which the night before he had heard the detective's stories of crimes and criminals had changed now to annoyance at the very sight of him. As a raconteur, Mr. Hastings was quite the thing; as protector of the Sloane family's privacy and seclusion, he was a nuisance. Such was the impression Mr. Hastings received.

At a loss to understand his host's frame of mind, he took a chair near the bed.

Mr. Sloane stirred jerkily under his thin summer coverings.

"A little light, Jarvis," he said peevishly. "Now, Mr. Hastings, what can I do for—tell you?"

Jarvis put back a curtain.

"Quivering and crucified martyrs!" the prostrate man burst forth. "I said a little, Jarvis! You drown my optic nerves in ink and, without a moment's warning, flood them with the glaring brilliancy of the noonday sun!" Jarvis half-drew the curtain. "Ah, that's better. Never more than an inch at a time, Jarvis. How many times have I told you that? Never give me a shock like that again; never more than an inch of light at a time. Frantic fiends! From cimmerian, abysmal darkness to Sahara-desert glare!"

"Yes, sir," said Jarvis, as if on the point of digging a grave—for himself. "Beg pardon, sir."

He effaced himself, in shadows, somewhere behind Hastings, who seized the opportunity to speak.

"Miss Sloane suggested that you wanted certain information. In fact, she asked me to see you."

"My daughter? Oh, yes!" The prone body became semi-upright, leaned on an elbow. "Yes! What I want to know is, why—why, in the name of all the jumping angels, everybody seems to think there's a lot of mystery connected with this brutal, vulgar, dastardly crime! It passes my comprehension, utterly!—Jarvis, stop clicking your finger-nails together!" This with a note of exaggerated pleading. "You know I'm a nervous wreck, a total loss physically, and yet you stand there in the corner and indulge yourself wickedly, wickedly, in that infernal habit of yours of clicking your finger-nails! Mute and mutilated Christian martyrs!"

He fell back among the pillows, breathing heavily, the perfect picture of exhaustion. Jarvis came near on soundless feet and applied a wet cloth to his master's temples.

The old man regarded them both with unconcealed amazement.

"You'll have to excuse me, Mr. Hastings, really, I can't be annoyed!" the wreck, somewhat revived, announced feebly. "All I said to my daughter, Miss Sloane, is what I say to you now: I see no reason why we should employ you, or indeed why you should be connected with this affair. You were my guest, here, at Sloanehurst. Unfortunately, some ruffian of whom we never heard, whose existence we never suspected—Jarvis, take off this counterpane; you're boiling me, parboiling me; my nerves are seething, simmering, stewing! Athletic devils! Have you no discrimination, Jarvis?—as I was saying, Mr. Hastings, somebody stabbed somebody else to death on my lawn, unfortunately marring your visit. But that's all. I can't see that we need you—thank you, nevertheless."

The dismissal was unequivocal. Hastings got to his feet, his indignation all the greater through realization that he had been sent for merely to be flouted. And yet, this man's daughter had come to him literally with tears in her eyes, had begged him to help her, had said that money was the smallest of considerations. Moreover, he had accepted her employment, had made the definite agreement and promise. Apparently, Sloane was in no condition to act independently, and his daughter had known it, had hoped that he, Hastings, might soothe his silly mind, do away with his objections to assistance which she knew he needed.

There was, also, the fact that Lucille believed her father unaccountably interested, if not implicated, in the crime. He could not get away from that impression. He was sure he had interpreted correctly the girl's anxiety the night before. She was working to save her father—from something. And she believed Berne Webster innocent.

These were some of the considerations which, flashing through his mind, prevented his giving way to righteous wrath. He most certainly would not allow Arthur Sloane to eliminate him from the situation. He sat down again.

The nervous wreck made himself more understandable.

"Perhaps, Jarvis," he said, shrinking to one side like a man in sudden pain, "the gentleman can't see how to reach that large door. A little more light, half an inch-not a fraction more!"

"Don't bother," Hastings told Jarvis. "I'm not going quite yet."

"Leaping crime!" moaned Mr. Sloane, digging deeper into the pillows, "Frantic imps!"

"I hope I won't distress you too much," the detective apologized grimly, "if I ask you a few questions. Fact is, I must. I'm investigating the circumstances surrounding what may turn out to be a baffling crime, and, irrespective of your personal wishes, Mr. Sloane, I can't let go of it. This is a serious business—"

The sick man sat up in bed with surprising abruptness.

"Serious business! Serious saints!—Jarvis, the eau de cologne!—You think I don't know it? They make a slaughter-house of my lawn. They make a morgue of my house. They hold a coroner's inquest in my parlour. They're in there now—live people like ravens, and one dead one. They cheat the undertaker to plague me. They wreck me all over again. They give me a new exhaustion of the nerves. They frighten my daughter to death.— Jarvis, the smelling salts. Shattered saints, Jarvis! Hurry! Thanks.—They rig up lies which, Tom Wilton, my old and trusted friend, tells me, will incriminate Berne Webster. They sit around a corpse in my house and chatter by the hour. You come in here and make Jarvis nearly blind me.

"And, then, then, by the holy, agile angels! you think you have to persuade me it's a serious business! Never fear! I know it!—Jarvis, the bromide, quick! Before I know it, they'll drive me to opiates.—Serious business! Shrivelled and shrinking saints!"

Arms clasped around his legs, knees pressed against his chin, Mr. Sloane trembled and shook until Jarvis, more agile than the angels of whom his employer had spoken, gave him the dose of bromides.

Still, Mr. Hastings did not retire.

"I was going to say," he resumed, in a tone devoid of compassion, "I couldn't drop this thing now. I may be able to find the murderer; and you may be able to help me."

"I?"

"Yes."

"Isn't it Russell? He's among the ravens now, in my parlour. Wilton told me the sheriff was certain Russell was the man. Murdered martyrs! Sacrificed saints! Can't you let a guilty man hang when he comes forward and puts the rope around his own worthless neck?"

"If Russell's guilty," Hastings said, glad of the information that the accused man was then at Sloanehurst, "I hope we can develop the necessary evidence against him. But—"

"The necessary—"

"Let me finish, Mr. Sloane, if you please!" The old man was determined to disregard the other's signs of suffering. He did not believe that they were anything but assumed, the exaggerated camouflage which he usually employed as an excuse for idleness. "But, if Russell isn't guilty, there are facts which may help me to find the murderer. And you may have valuable information concerning them."

"Sobbing, sorrowing saints!" lamented Mr. Sloane, but his trembling ceased; he was closely attentive. "A cigarette, Jarvis, a cigarette! Nerves will be served.—I suppose the easiest way is to submit. Go on."

"I shall ask you only two or three questions," Hastings said.

The jackknife-like figure in the bed shuddered its repugnance.

"I've been told, Mr. Sloane, that Mr. Webster has been in great need of money, as much as sixty-five thousand dollars. In fact, according to my information, he needs it now."

"Well, did he kill the woman, expecting to find it in her stocking?"

"The significance of his being hard-pressed, for so large an amount," the old man went on, ignoring the sarcasm, "is in the further charge that Miss Brace was trying to make him marry her, that he should have married her, that he killed her in order to be free to marry your daughter—for money."

"My daughter! For money!" shrilled Sloane, neck elongated, head thrust forward, eyes bulging. "Leaping and whistling cherubim!" For all his outward agitation, he seemed to Hastings in thorough command of his logical faculties; it was more than possible, the detective thought, that the expletives were time-killers, until he could decide what to say. "It's ridiculous, absurd! Why, sir, you reason as loosely as you dress! Are you trying to prostrate me further with impossible theories? Webster marry my daughter for money, for sixty-five thousand dollars? He knows I'd let him have any amount he wanted. I'd give him the money if it meant his peace of mind and Lucille's happiness.—Dumb and dancing devils! Jarvis, a little whiskey! I'm worn out, worn out!"

"Did you ever tell Mr. Webster of the extent of your generous feeling toward him, Mr. Sloane—in dollars and cents?"

"No; it wasn't necessary. He knows how fond of him I am."

"And you would let him have sixty-five thousand dollars—if he had to have it?"

"I would, sir!—today, this morning."

"Now, one other thing, Mr. Sloane, and I'm through. It's barely possible that there was some connection between this murder and a letter which came to Sloanehurst yesterday afternoon, a letter in an oblong grey envelope. Did—"

The nervous man went to pieces again, beat with his open palms on the bed covering.

"Starved and stoned evangels, Jarvis! Quit balling your feet! You stand there and see me harassed to the point of extinction by a lot of crazy queries, and you indulge yourself in that infernal weakness of yours of balling your feet! Leaping angels! You know how acute my hearing is; you know the noise of your sock against the sole of your shoe when you ball your feet is the most exquisite torture to me! A little whiskey, Jarvis! Quick!" He spoke now in a weak, almost inaudible voice to Hastings: "No; I got no such letter. I saw no such letter." He sank slowly back to a prone posture.

"I was going to remind you," the detective continued, "that I brought the five o'clock mail in. Getting off the car, I met the rural carrier; he asked me to bring in the mail, saving him the few steps to your box. All there was consisted of a newspaper and one letter. I recall the shape and colour of the envelope—oblong, grey. I did not, of course, look at the address. I handed the mail to you when you met me on the porch."

Mr. Sloane, raising himself on one elbow to take the restoring drink from Jarvis, looked across the glass at his cross-examiner.

"I put the mail in the basket on the hall table," he said in high-keyed endeavour to express withering contempt. "If it had been for me, Jarvis would have brought it to me later. I seldom carry my reading glasses about the house with me."

Hastings, subjecting the pallid Jarvis to severe scrutiny, asked him:

"Was that grey letter addressed to—whom?"

"I didn't see it," replied Jarvis, scarcely polite.

"And yet, it's your business to inspect and deliver the household's mail?"

"Yes, sir."

"What became of it, then—the grey envelope?"

"I'm sure I can't say, sir, unless some one got it before I reached the mail basket."

Hastings stood up. Interrogation of both master and man had given him nothing save the inescapable conviction that both of them resented his questioning and would do nothing to help him. The reason for this opposition he could not grasp, but it was a fact, challenging his analysis. Arthur Sloane rejected his proffered help in the pursuit of the man who had brought murder to the doors of Sloanehurst. Why? Was this his method of hiding facts in his possession?

Hastings questioned him again:

"Your waking up at that unusual hour last night—was it because of a noise outside?"

The neurasthenic, once more recumbent, succeeded in voicing faint denial of having heard any noises, outside or inside. Nor had he been aware of the murder until called by Judge Wilton. He had turned on his light to find the smelling-salts which, for the first time in six years, Jarvis had failed to leave on his bed-table,—terrible and ill-trained apes! Couldn't he be left in peace?

The hall door opened, admitting Judge Wilton. The newcomer, with a word of greeting to Hastings, sat down on the bedside and put a hand on Sloane's shoulder.

Hastings turned to leave the room.

"Any news?" the judge asked him.

"I've just been asking Mr. Sloane that," Hastings said, in a tone that made Wilton look swiftly at his friend's face.

"I told Arthur this morning," he said, "how lucky he was that you'd promised Lucille to go into this thing."

"Apparently," Hastings retorted drily, "he's unconvinced of the extent of his good fortune."

Mr. Sloane, quivering from head to foot, mourned softly: "Unfathomable fate!"

Wilton, his rugged features softening to frank amusement, stared a moment in silence at Sloane's thin face, at the deeply lined forehead topped by stringy grey hair.

"See here, Arthur," he protested, nodding Hastings an invitation to remain; "you know as much about crime as Hastings and I. If you've thought about this murder at all, you must see what it is. If Russell isn't guilty—if he's not the man, that crime was committed shrewdly, with forethought. And it was a devilish thing—devilish!"

"Well, what of it?" Sloane protested shrilly, not opening his eyes.

"Take my advice. Quit antagonizing Mr. Hastings. Be thankful that he's here, that he's promised to run down the guilty man."

Mr. Sloane turned his face to the wall.

"A little whiskey, Jarvis," he said softly. "I'm exhausted, Tom. Leave me alone."

Wilton waved his hand, indicative of the futility of further argument.

"Judge," announced Hastings, at the door, "I'll ask you a question I put to Mr. Sloane. Did you receive, or see, a letter in an oblong, grey envelope in yesterday afternoon's mail?"

"No. I never get any mail while I'm here for a week-end."

Wilton followed the detective into the hall.

"I hope you're not going to give up the case, Hastings. You won't pay any attention to Arthur's unreasonable attitude, will you?"

"I don't know," Hastings said, still indignant. "I made my bargain with his daughter. I'll see her."

"If you can't manage any other way, I—or she—will get any information you want from Arthur."

"I hope to keep on. It's a big thing, I think." The old man was again intent on solving the problem. "Tell me, judge; do you think Berne Webster's guilty?" Seeing the judge's hesitance, he supplemented: "I mean, did you notice anything last night, in his conduct, that would indicate guilt—or fear?"

Later, when other developments gave this scene immense importance, Hastings, in reviewing it, remembered the curious little flicker of the judge's eyelids preceding his reply.

"Absolutely not," he declared, with emphasis. "Are you working on that"—he hesitated hardly perceptibly—"idea?"

VIII
The Man Who Ran Away

Ancestors of the old family from whom Arthur Sloane had purchased this colonial mansion eight years ago still looked out of their gilded frames on the parlour walls, their high-bred calm undisturbed, their aristocratic eyes unwidened, by the chatter and clatter of the strangers within their gates. Hastings noticed that even the mob and mouthing of a coroner's inquest failed to destroy the ancient atmosphere and charm of the great room. He smiled. The pictured grandeur of a bygone age, the brocaded mahogany chairs, the tall French mirrors—all these made an incongruous setting for the harsh machinery of crime-inquiry.

The detective had completed his second and more detailed search of the guest-rooms in time to hear the words and study the face of the last witness on Dr. Garnet's list. That was Eugene Russell.

"One of life's persimmons—long before frost!" Hastings thought, making swift appraisal. "A boneless spine—chin like a sheep—brave as a lamb."

Russell could not conceal his agitation. In fact, he referred to it. Fear, he explained in a low, husky voice to the coroner and the jury, was not a part of his emotions. His only feeling was sorrow, varied now and then by the embarrassment he felt as a result of the purely personal and very intimate facts which he had to reveal.

His one desire was to be frank, he declared, his pale blue eyes roving from place to place, his nervous fingers incessantly playing with his thin, uncertain lips. This mania for truthfulness, he asserted, was natural, in that it offered him the one sure path to freedom and the establishment of his innocence of all connection with the murder of the woman he had loved.

He was, he testified, thirty-one years old, a clerk in a real-estate dealer's office and a native of Washington. Mildred Brace had been employed for a few weeks by the same firm for which he worked, and it was there that he had met her. Although she had refused to marry him on the ground that his salary was inadequate for the needs of two people, she had encouraged his attentions. Sometimes, they had quarrelled.

"Speak up, Mr. Russell!" Dr. Garnet directed. "And take your time. Let the jury hear every word you utter."

After that, the witness abandoned his attempt to exclude the family portraits from his confidence, but his voice shook.

"Conductor Barton is right," he said, responding to the coroner's interrogation. "I did come out on his car, the car that gets to the Sloanehurst stop at ten-thirty, and I did leave the car at the Ridgecrest stop, a quarter of a mile from here. I was following Mil—Miss Brace. I saw her leave her apartment house, the Walman. I followed her to the transfer station at the bridge, and I saw her take the car there. I followed on the next car. I knew where she was going, knew she was going to Sloanehurst."

"How did you know that, Mr. Russell?"

"I mean I was certain of it. She'd told me Mr. Berne Webster, the lawyer she'd been working for, was out here spending the week-end; and I knew she was coming out to meet him."

"Why did she do that?"

Mr. Russell displayed pathetic embarrassment and confusion before he answered that. He plucked at his lower lip with spasmodic fingers. His eyes were downcast. He attempted a self-deprecatory smile which ended in an unpleasant grimace.

"She wouldn't say. But it was because she was in love with him."

"And you were jealous of Mr. Webster?"

"We-ell—yes, sir; that's about it, I guess."

"Did Miss Brace tell you she was coming to Sloanehurst?"

"No, sir. I suspected it."

"And watched her movements?"

"Yes, sir."

"And followed her?"

"Yes."

"Why did you think she was in love with Mr. Webster, Mr. Russell? And please give us a direct answer. You can understand the importance of what you're about to say."

"I do. I thought so because she had told me that he was in love with her, and because of her grief and anger when he dismissed her from his office. And she did everything to make me think so, except declaring it outright. She did that because she knew I hated to think she was in love with him."

"All right, Mr. Russell. Now, tell us what happened during your—ah—shadowing Miss Brace the night she was killed."

"I got off the car at Ridgecrest and walked toward Sloanehurst. It was raining then, pretty hard. I thought she had made an appointment to meet Mr. Webster somewhere in the grounds here. It was a quarter to eleven when I got to the little side-gate that opens on the lawn out there on the north side of the house."

"How did you know that?"

"I looked at my watch then. It's got a luminous dial."

"You were then at the gate near where she was found, dead?"

"Yes. And she was at the gate."

"Oh! So you saw her?"

"I saw her. When I lifted the latch of the gate, she came toward me. There was a heavy drizzle then. I thought she had been leaning on the fence a few feet away. She whispered, sharp and quick, 'Who's that?' I knew who she was, right off. I said, 'Gene.'

"She caught hold of my arm and shook it. She told me, still whispering, if I didn't get away from there, if I didn't go back to town, she'd raise an alarm, accuse me of trying to kill her—or she'd kill me. She pressed something against my cheek. It felt like a knife, although I couldn't see, for the darkness."

The witness paused and licked his dry lips. He was breathing fast, and his restless eyes had a hunted look. The people in the room leaned farther toward him, some believing, some doubting him.

Hastings thought: "He's scared stiff, but telling the truth—so far."

"All right; what next?" asked Dr. Garnet, involuntarily lowering his voice to Russell's tone.

"I accused her of having an appointment to meet Webster there. I got mad. I hate to have to tell all this, gentlemen; but I want to tell the truth. I told her she was a fool to run after a man who'd thrown her over.

"'It's none of your look-out what I do!' she told me. 'You get away from here, now—this minute! You'll be sorry if you don't!' There was something about her that frightened me, mad as I was. I'd never seen her like that before."

"What do you mean?" Garnet urged him.

"I thought she would kill me, or somebody else would, and she knew it. I got the idea that she was like a crazy woman, out of her head about Webster, ready to do anything desperate, anything wild. I can't explain it any better than that."

"And did you leave her?"

"Yes, sir."

"At once?"

"Practically. A sort of panic got hold of me. I can't explain it, really."

Russell, seeking an illuminative phrase, gave vent to a long-drawn, anxious sigh. He appeared to feel no shame for his flight. His fear was that he would not be believed.

"Just as she told me a second time to leave her, I thought I heard somebody coming toward us, a slushy, dull sound, like heavy footsteps on the wet grass. Mildred's manner, her voice, had already scared me.

"When I heard those footsteps, I turned and ran. My heart was in my mouth. I ran out to the road and back toward Washington. I ran as fast as I could. Twice I fell on my hands and knees. I can't tell you exactly how it was, why it was. I just knew something terrible would happen if I stayed there. I never had a feeling like that before. I was more afraid of her than I was of the man coming toward us."

Members of the jury pushed back their chairs, were audible with subdued exclamations and long breaths, relieved of the nervous tension to which Russell's story of the encounter at the gate had lifted them. They were, however, prejudiced against him, a fact which he grasped.

One of them asked him:

"Can you tell us why you followed her out here?"

"Why?" Russell echoed, like a man seeking time for deliberation.

"Yes. What did you think you'd do after you'd overtaken her?"

"Persuade her to go back home with me. I wanted to save her from doing anything foolish—anything like that, you know."

"But, from what you've told us here this morning, it seems you never had much influence on her behaviour. Isn't that true?"

"I suppose it is.—But," Russell added eagerly, "I can prove I had no idea of hurting her, if that's what you're hinting at. I can prove I never struck her. At twenty minutes past eleven last night I was four miles from here. Mr. Otis, a Washington commission merchant, picked me up in his automobile, six miles outside of Washington and took me into town. I couldn't have made that four miles on foot, no matter how I ran, in approximately fifteen or twenty minutes.

"It's been proved that she was struck down after eleven anyway.—You said the condition of the body showed that, doctor.—You see, I would have had to make the four miles in less than twenty minutes—an impossibility. You see?"

His eagerness to win their confidence put a disagreeable note, almost a whimper, into his voice. It grated on Dr. Garnet.

It affected Hastings more definitely.

"Now," he decided, "he's lying—about something. But what?" He noted a change in Russell's face, a suggestion of craftiness, the merest shadow of slyness over his general attitude of anxiety. And yet, this part of his story seemed straight enough.

Dr. Garnet's next question brought out the fact that it would be corroborated.

"This Mr. Otis, Mr. Russell; where is he?"

"Right there, by the window," the witness answered, with a smug smile which gave him a still more unprepossessing look.

Jury and spectators turned toward the man at the window. They saw a clean-shaven, alert-looking person of middle age, who nodded slightly in

Russell's direction as if endorsing his testimony. There seemed no possible grounds for doubting whatever Otis might say. Hastings at once accepted him as genuine, an opinion which, it was obvious, was shared by the rest of the assemblage.

Russell sensed the change of sentiment toward himself. Until now, it had been a certainty that he would be held for the murder. But his producing an outsider, incontestably a trustworthy man, to establish the truth of his statement that he had been four miles away from the scene of the crime a quarter of an hour after it had been committed—that was something in his favour which could not be gainsaid.

Granting even that he had had an automobile at his disposal—a supposition for which there was no foundation—his alibi would still have been good, in view of the rain and the fact that one of the four miles in question was "dirt road."

With the realization of this, the jury swung back to the animus it had felt against Webster, the incredulity with which it had received his statement that there had been between him and the dead woman no closer relationship than that of employer and employe.

Webster, seated near the wall furthest from the jury, felt the inquiry of many eyes upon him, but he was unmoved, kept his gaze on Russell.

Dr. Garnet, announcing that he would ask Mr. Otis to testify a little later, handed Russell the weapon with which Mildred Brace had been murdered.

"Have you ever seen that dagger before?" he asked.

Russell said he had not. Reminded that Sheriff Crown had testified to searching the witness's room and had discovered that a nail file was missing from his dressing case, a file which, judging by other articles in the case, must have been the same size as the one used in making the amateur dagger, Russell declared that his file had been lost for three years. He had left it in a hotel room on the only trip he had ever taken to New York.

He gave way to Mr. Otis, who described himself as a commission merchant of Washington. Returning from a tour to Lynchburg, Virginia, he said, he had been hailed last night by a man in the road and had agreed to take him into town, a ride of six miles. Reaching Washington shortly before midnight, he had dropped his passenger at Eleventh and F streets.

"Who was this passenger?" inquired Garnet.

"He told me," said Otis, "his name was Eugene Russell. I gave him my name. That explains how he was able to find me this morning. When he told me how he was situated, I agreed to come over here and give you gentlemen the facts."

"Notice anything peculiar about Mr. Russell last night?"

"No; I think not."

"Was he agitated, disturbed?"

"He was out of breath. And he commented on that himself, said he'd been walking fast. Oh, yes! He was bareheaded; and he explained that— said the rain had ruined a cheap straw hat he had been wearing; the glue had run out of the straw and down his neck, he had thrown the hat away."

"And the time? When did you pick him up?"

"It was twenty minutes past eleven o'clock. When I stopped, I glanced at my machine clock; I carry a clock just above my speedometer."

Mr. Otis was positive in his statements. He realized, he said, that his words might relieve one man of suspicion and bring it upon another. Unless he had been absolutely certain of his facts, he would not have stated them. He was sure, beyond the possibility of doubt, that he had made no mistake when he looked at his automobile clock; it was running when he stopped and when he reached Washington; yes, it was an accurate timepiece.

Russell's alibi was established. His defence appealed to the jurymen as unassailable. When, after a conference of less than half an hour, they brought in a verdict that Mildred Brace had been murdered by a thrust of the "nail-file dagger" in the hands of a person unknown, nobody in the room was surprised.

And nobody was blind to the fact that the freeing of Eugene Russell seriously questioned the innocence of Berne Webster.

IX

The Breaking Down of Webster

Hastings, sprawling comfortably in a low chair by the south window in the music room, stopped his whittling when Berne Webster came in with Judge Wilton. "Meddlesome Mike!" thought the detective. "I sent for Webster."

"Berne asked me to come with him," the judge explained his presence at once. "We've talked things over; he thought I might help him bring out every detail—jog his memory, if necessary."

Hastings did not protest the arrangement. He saw, almost immediately, that Webster had come with no intention of giving him hearty cooperation. The motive for this lack of frankness he could not determine. It was enough that he felt the younger man's veiled antagonism and appreciated the fact that Wilton accompanied him in the rôle of protector.

"If I'm to get anything worth while out of this talk," he decided, "I've got to mix up my delivery, shuffle the cards, spring first one thing and then another at him—bewilder him."

He proceeded with that definite design: at an opportune time, he would guide the narrative, take it out of Webster's hands, and find out what he wanted to know, not merely what the young lawyer wanted to tell. He recognized the necessity of breaking down the shell of self-control that overlaid the suspected man's uneasiness.

That it was only a shell, he felt sure. Webster, leaning an elbow lightly on the piano, looked down at him out of anxious eyes, and continually passed his right hand over his smooth, dark-brown hair from forehead to crown, a mechanical gesture of his when perplexed.

His smile, too, was forced, hardly more than a slight, fixed twist of the lips, as if he strove to advertise his ability to laugh at danger. His customary dash, a pleasing levity of manner, was gone, giving place to a suggestion of strain, so that he seemed always on the alert against himself, determined to edit in advance his answer to every question.

Wilton had chosen a chair which placed him directly opposite Hastings and at the same time enabled him to watch Webster. He was smoking a cigar, and, through the haze that floated up just then from his lips, he gave the detective a long, searching look, to which Hastings paid no attention.

Webster talked nearly twenty minutes, explaining his eagerness to be "thoroughly frank as to every detail," reviewing the evidence brought out by the inquest, and criticising the action of the jury, but producing nothing new. Occasionally he left the piano and paced the floor, smoking interminably, lighting the fresh cigarette from the stub of the old, obviously strung to the limit of his nervous strength. Hastings detected a little twitching of the muscles at the corners of his mouth, and the too frequent winking of his eyes.

Judge Wilton had told him, Webster continued, of Mrs. Brace's charge that he wanted to marry Miss Sloane because of financial pressure; there was not a word of truth in it; he had already arranged for a loan to make that payment when it fell due. He was, however, aware of his unenviable position, and he wanted to give the detective every assistance possible, in that way assuring his own prompt relief from embarrassment.

By this time, Hastings had mapped out his line of questioning, his assault on Webster's reticence.

"That's the right idea!" he said, getting to his feet. "Let's go to work."

They saw the change in him. Instead of the genial, drawling, slow-moving old fellow who had seemed thankful for anything he might chance to hear, they were confronted now by an aroused, quick-thinking man whose words came from him with a sharp, clipped-off effect, and whose questions scouted the whole field of their possible and probable information. He stood leaning his elbows on the other end of the piano, facing Webster across the polished length of its broad top. His dominance of the night before, in the library, had returned.

"Now, Mr. Webster," he began, innocent of threat, "as things stack up at present, only two people had the semblance of a motive for killing Mildred Brace—either Eugene Russell killed her out of jealousy of you; or you killed her to silence her demands. Do you see that?"

He had put back his head a little and was peering at Webster under his spectacle-rims, down the line of his nose. He saw how the other fought down the impulse to deny, hesitating before answering, with a laugh on a high note, like derision:

"I suppose that's what a lot of people will say."

"Precisely. Now, I've just had a talk with this Russell—caught him after the inquest. I believe there's something rotten about that alibi of his; but I couldn't shake him; and the Otis testimony's sound. So we'll have to quit counting on Russell's proving his own guilt. We've got that little job on our hands, and the best way to handle it is to prove your innocence. See that?"

The bow with which Webster acknowledged this statement was a curious mingling of grace and mockery. The detective ignored it.

"And," he continued, "there's only one way for you to come whole out of this muddle—frankness. I'm working for you; you know that. Tell me everything you know, and we've got a chance to win. The innocent man who tries to twist black into white is an innocent fool." He looked swiftly to Wilton, who was leaning far back in his chair, head lolling slowly from side to side, the picture of indifference. "Isn't that so, judge?"

"Quite," Wilton agreed, pausing to remove his cigar from his mouth.

"Of course, it's so," Webster said curtly. "I've just told you so. That's why I've decided—the judge and I have talked it over—to give you something in confidence."

"One moment!" Hastings warned him. "Maybe, I won't take it in confidence—if it's something incriminating you."

"Yes; you've phrased that unfortunately, Berne," the judge put in, tilting his head on the chair-back to meet the detective's look.

Webster was nonplussed. Apparently, his surprise came from the judge's remark rather than from the detective's refusal to assume the rôle of confidant. Hastings inferred that Wilton, agreeing beforehand to the proposal being advanced, had changed his mind after entering the room.

"Hastings is right," the judge concluded; "even if he's on your side, you can't expect him to be tied up blind that way by a suspected man—and you're just that, Berne."

Seeing Webster's uncertainty, Hastings took another course.

"I think I know what you're talking about, Mr. Webster," he said, matter-of-fact. "Your nail-file's missing from your dressing case—disappeared since yesterday morning."

"You know that!" Berne flashed, suddenly angry. "And you're holding it over me!"

Open hostility was in every feature of his face; his lips twitched to the sharp intake of his breath.

"Why don't you look at it another way?" the old man countered quickly. "If I'd told the coroner about it—if I'd told him also that the size of that nail-file, judging from the rest of the dressing case, matched that of the one used for the blade of the dagger, matched it as well as Russell's—what then?"

"He's right, Berne," Wilton cautioned again. "He's taken the friendly course."

"I understand that, judge," Berne said; and, without answering Hastings, turned squarely to Wilton: "But it's a thin clue. He admits Russell lost a nail-file, too."

"Several years ago," Hastings goaded, so that Webster pivoted on his heel to face him; "you lost yours when?—last night?—this morning?"

"I don't know! I noticed its absence this morning."

"There you are!—But," Hastings qualified, to avoid the quarrel, "the nail-file isn't much of a clue if unsupported." He approached cordiality. "And I appreciate your intending to tell me. That was what you intended to give me in confidence, wasn't it?"

"Yes," Webster answered, half-sullen.

Hastings changed the subject again.

"Did you know Mildred Brace intended to clear out, leave Washington, today?"

"Why, no!" Webster shot that out in genuine surprise.

"I got it from Russell," Hastings informed, and went at once to another topic.

"And that brings us to the letter. Judge Wilton tell you about that?"

Webster was lighting a cigarette, with difficulty holding the fire of the old one to the end of the new. The operation seemed to entail hard labour for him.

"In the grey envelope?" he responded, drawing on the cigarette. "Yes. I didn't get it."

He took off his coat. The heat oppressed him. At frequent intervals he passed his handkerchief around the inside of his collar, which was wilting. Now, more than ever, he gave the impression of exaggerated watchfulness, as if he attempted prevision of the detective's questions.

"Nobody got it, so far as I can learn," Hastings said, a note of sternness breaking through the surface of his tone. "It vanished into thin air. That's the most mysterious thing about this mysterious murder."

He, in his turn, began pacing the floor, a short distance to and fro in front of Judge Wilton's chair, his hands behind him, flopping the baggy tail of his coat from side to side.

"You doubtless see the gravity of the facts: that letter was mailed to Sloanehurst. Russell has just told me so. She waved it in his face, to taunt him about you, before she dropped it into the mail-box. He swears"—Hastings stopped, at the far end of his pacing, and looked hard at Webster—"it was addressed to you."

Webster, again with his queer, high-pitched laugh, like derision, threw back his head and took two long strides toward the centre of the room. There he stood a moment, hands in his pockets, while he stared at the toe of his right shoe, which he was carefully adjusting to a crack in the flooring.

Judge Wilton made his chair crackle as he moved to look at Webster. It was the weight of the detective's gaze, however, that drew the lawyer's attention; when he looked up, his eyes were half-closed, as if the light had suddenly become painful to them.

"That would be Russell's game, wouldn't it?" he retorted, at last.

"Mrs. Brace told me the same thing," Hastings said quietly, flashing a look at Wilton and back to the other.

"Damn her!" Webster broke forth with such vehemence that Wilton stared at him in amazement. "Damn her! And that's the first time I ever said that of a woman. It's as I suspected, as I expected. She's begun some sort of a crooked game!"

He trembled like a man with a chill. Hastings gave him no time to recover himself.

"You know Mrs. Brace, then? Know her well?" he pressed.

"Well enough!" Webster retorted with hot repugnance. "Well enough, although I never had but one conversation with her—if you may call that bedlam wildness a conversation. She came to my office the second day after I'd dismissed her daughter. She made a scene. She charged me with ruining her daughter's life, threatened suit for breach of promise. She said she'd 'get even' with me if it took her the rest of her life. I don't as a rule pay much attention to violent women, Mr. Hastings; but there was something about her that affected me strongly, she's implacable, and like stone, not like a woman. You saw her—understand what I mean?"

"Perfectly," agreed Hastings.

There flashed across his mind a picture of that incomprehensible woman's face, the black line of her eyebrows lifted half-way to her hair, the abnormal wetness of her lips thickened by a sneer. "If she's been after this man for two weeks," he thought, "I can understand his trembles!"

But he hurried the inquiry.

"So you think she lied about that letter?"

"Of course!" Webster laughed on a high note. "Next, I suppose, she'll produce the letter."

"She can't very well do that."

Something in his voice alarmed the suspected man.

"What do you mean?" he asked.

Hastings smiled.

"What do you mean?" Webster asked again, his voice lowered, and came a step nearer to the detective.

Hastings took a piece of paper from his pocket.

"Here's the flap of the grey envelope," he said, as if that was all the information he meant to impart.

Webster urged him, with eyes and voice:

"Well?"

"And on the back of it is some of Mildred Brace's handwriting."

The old man examined the piece of paper with every show of absorption. He could hear Webster's hurried breathing, and the gulp when he swallowed the lump in his throat.

The scene had got hold of Wilton also. Leaning forward in his chair, his lips half-parted, the thumb and forefinger of his right hand mechanically fubbing out his cigar, so that a little stream of fire trickled to the floor, he gazed unwinking at the envelope flap.

Webster went a step nearer to Hastings, and stood, passing his hand across the top of his head and staring again out of his half-closed eyes, as if the light had hurt them.

"And," the old man said, regarding Webster keenly but keeping any hint of accusation out of his voice, "I found it last night in the fireplace, behind the screen, in your room upstairs."

He paused, looking toward the door, his attention caught by a noise in the hall.

Webster laughed, on the high, derisive note. He was noticeably pale.

"Come, man!" Judge Wilton said, harsh and imperious. "Can't you see the boy's suffering? What's written on it?"

"What difference does it make—the writing?" Webster objected, with a movement of his shoulders that looked like a great effort to pull himself together. "If there's any at all, it's faked. Faked! That's what it is. People don't write on the inside of envelope flaps."

His face did not express the assurance he tried to put into his voice. He went back to the piano and leaned on it, his posture such that it might have indicated a nonchalant ease or, equally well, might have betrayed his desperate need of support.

"This letter incident can't be waved away," Hastings, without handing over the scrap of envelope, proceeded in even, measured tones—using his sentences as if they were hammers with which he assailed the young lawyer's remnants of self-control. "You're not trifling with a jury, Mr. Webster. I believe I know as much about the value of facts, this kind of facts, as you do. Consider what you're up against. You—"

Webster put up a hand in protest, the fingers so unsteady that they dropped the cigarette which he had been on the point of lighting.

"Just a moment!" the old man commanded him. "This Mildred Brace claimed she had suffered injury at your hands. You fired her out of your office. She and her mother afterwards pursued you. She came out here in the middle of the night, where she knew you were. She was murdered, and by a weapon whose blade may have been fashioned from an article you possessed, an article which is now missing, missing since you came to Sloanehurst this time. You were found bending over the dead body.

"Her mother and her closest friend, her would-be fiancé, say she wrote to you Friday night, addressing her letter to Sloanehurst. The flap of an envelope, identified by her mother and friend, and bearing the impression in ink of her handwriting, is found in the fireplace of your room here. The man who followed her out here, who might have been suspected of the murder, has proved an alibi.

"Now, I ask you, as a lawyer and a sensible man, who's going to believe that she came out here without having notified you of her coming? Who, as facts stand now, is going to believe anything but that you, desperate with the fear that she would make revelations which would prevent your marriage to Miss Sloane and keep you from access to an immense amount of money which you needed—who's going to believe you didn't kill her, didn't strike her down, there in the night, according to a premeditated plan, with a dagger which, for better protection of yourself, you had manufactured in a way which you hoped would make it beyond identification? Who's—"

Wilton intervened again.

"What's your object, Hastings?" he demanded, springing from his chair. "You're treating Berne as if he'd killed the woman and you could prove it!"

Webster was swaying on his feet, falling a little away from the piano and reeling against it again, his elbows sliding back and forth on its top. He was extremely pale; even his lips, still stiff and twisted to what he thought was a belittling smile, were white. He looked at the detective as a man might gaze at an advancing terror which he could neither resist nor flee. His going to pieces was so complete, so absolute, that it astonished Hastings.

"And you, both of you," the old man retorted to Wilton's protest; "you're treating me as if I were a meddlesome outsider intent on 'framing up' a case, instead of the representative of the Sloane family—at least, of Miss Lucille Sloane! Why's that?"

"Tell me what's on that paper," Webster said hoarsely, as if he had not heard the colloquy of the other two.

He held up a trembling hand, but without taking a step. He still swayed, like a man dangled on strings, against the piano.

"Yes; tell him!" urged Wilton.

Hastings handed Webster the envelope flap. Instead of looking at it, Webster let it drop on the piano.

"One of the words," Hastings said, "is 'pursuit.' The other two are uncompleted."

"And it's her handwriting, the daughter's?" Wilton said.

"Beyond a doubt."

Webster kept his unwinking eyes on the detective, apparently unable to break the spell that held him. For a long moment, he had said nothing. When he did speak, it was with manifest difficulty. His words came in a screaming whisper:

"Then, I'm in desperate shape!"

"Nonsense, man!" Judge Wilton protested, his voice raised, and, going to his side, struck him sharply between the shoulders. "Get yourself together, Berne! Brace up!"

The effect on the collapsing man was, in a way, magical. He stood erect in response to the blow, his elbows no longer seeking support on the piano. He got his eyes away from Hastings and looked at the judge as a man coming out of a sound sleep might have done. For a few seconds, he had one hand over his mouth, as if, by actual manipulation, he would gain control of the muscles of his lips.

"I feel better," he said at last, dropping the hand from before his face and squaring his shoulders. "I don't know what hit me. If I'd—you know," he hesitated, frowning, "if I'd killed the woman, I couldn't have acted the coward more thoroughly."

Hastings went through with what he wanted to say:

"About that letter, Mr. Webster: have you any idea, can you advance any theory, as to how that piece of the envelope got into your room?"

Webster was passing his hand across his hair now, and breathing in a deep, gusty fashion.

"Not the faintest," he replied, hoarsely.

"That's all, then, gentlemen!" Hastings said, so abruptly that both of them started. "We don't seem to have gone very far ahead with this business. We won't, until you—particularly you, Webster—tell me what you know. It's your own affair—"

"My dear sir—" Judge Wilton began.

"Let me finish!" Hastings spoke indignantly. "I'm no fool; I know when I'm trifled with. Understand me: I don't say you got that letter, Mr. Webster; I don't say you ever saw it; I don't know the truth of it—yet. I do say you've deliberately refused to respond to my requests for cooperation. I do say you'd prefer to have me out of this case altogether. I know it, although I'm not clear as to your motives—or yours, judge. You were anxious enough, you said when we talked at Sloane's door, for me to go on with it. If you're still of that opinion, I advise you to advise your friend here to be more outspoken with me. I'll give you this straight: if I can't be corn, I won't be shucks. But I intend to be corn. I'm going to conduct this investigation as I see fit. I won't be turned aside; I won't play second to your lead!"

He was fine in his intensity. Astounded by his vehemence, the two men he addressed were silent, meeting his keen and steady scrutiny.

He smiled, and, as he did so, they were aware, with an emotion like shock, that his whole face mirrored forth a genuine and warm self-satisfaction. The thing was as plain as if he had spoken it aloud: he had gotten out of the interview what he wanted. Their recognition of this fact increased their blankness.

"You know my position now," he added, no longer denunciatory. "If you change your minds, that will be great! I want all the help I can get. And, take it from me, young man, you can't afford to throw away any you can get."

"Threats?"

Webster had shot out the one word with cool insolence before the judge could begin a conciliatory remark. The change in the lawyer's manner was so unpleasant, the insult so palpably deliberate, that Hastings could not mistake the purpose back of it. Webster regarded him out of burning eyes.

"No; not threats," Hastings answered him in a voice that was cold as ice. "I think you understand what I mean. I know too little, and I suspect too much, to drop my search for the murderer of that woman."

Judge Wilton tried to placate him:

"I don't see what your complaint is, Hastings. We—"

A smothered, half-articulate cry from Webster interrupted him. Hastings, first to spring forward, caught the falling man by his arm, breaking the force of the fall. He had clutched the edge of the piano as his legs gave under him. That, and the quickness of the detective, made the fall more like a gentle sliding to the floor.

Save for the one, gurgling outcry, no word came from him. He was unconscious, his colourless lips again twisted to that poor semblance of smiling defiance which Hastings had noticed at the beginning of the interview.

X

The Whispered Conference

Dr. Garnet, reaching Sloanehurst half an hour later, found Webster in complete collapse. He declared that for at least several days the sick man must be kept quiet. He could not be moved to his apartment in Washington, nor could he be subjected to questioning about anything.

"That is," he explained, "for three or four days—possibly longer. He's critically ill. But for my knowledge of the terrific shock he's sustained as a result of the murder, I'd be inclined to say he'd broken down after a long, steady nervous strain.

"I'll have a nurse out to look after him. Miss Sloane has volunteered, but she has troubles of her own."

Judge Wilton took the news to Hastings, who was on the front porch, whittling, waiting to see Lucille before returning to Washington.

"I think Garnet's right," Wilton added. "I thought, even before last night, Berne acted as if he'd been worn out. And you handled him rather roughly. That sort of questioning, tantalizing, keeping a man on tenterhooks, knocks the metal out of a high-strung temperament like his. I don't mind telling you it had me pretty well worked up."

"I'm sorry it knocked him out," Hastings said. "All I wanted was the facts. He wasn't frank with me."

"I came out here to talk about that," Wilton retorted, brusquely. "You're all wrong there, Hastings! The boy's broken all to pieces. He sees clearly, too clearly, the weight of suspicion against him. You've mistaken his panic for hostility toward yourself."

The old man was unconvinced, and showed it.

"Suspicion doesn't usually knock a man into a cocked hat—unless there's something to base it on," he contended.

"All right; I give up," Wilton said, with a short laugh. "All I know is, he came to me before we saw you in the music room, and told me he wanted me to be there, to see that he omitted not even a detail of what he knew."

Hastings, looking up from the intricate pattern he was carving, challenged the judge:

"Has it occurred to you that, if he's not guilty, he might suspect somebody else in this house, might be trying to shield that person?"

In the inconsiderable pause that followed, Wilton's lips, parting for an incredulous smile, showed the top of his tongue against his teeth, as if set for pronunciation of the letter "S." Hastings, in a mental flash, saw him on the point of exclaiming: "Sloane!" But, if that was in his mind, he put it down, elaborating the smile to a laughing protest:

"That's going far afield, isn't it?"

Hastings smiled in return: "Maybe so, but it's a possibility—and possibilities have to be dealt with."

"Which reminds me," the judge said, now all amiability; "don't forget I'm always at your service in this affair. I see now that you might have preferred to question Webster alone, in the music room; but my confidence in his innocence blinded me to the fact that you could regard him as actually guilty. I expected nothing but a friendly conference, not a fierce cross-examination."

"It didn't matter at all," Hastings matched Wilton's cordial tone; "and I appreciate your offer, judge. Suppose you tell me anything that occurs to you, anything that will throw light on this case any time; and I'll act as go-between for you with the authorities—if necessary."

"You mean—?"

"I'd like to do the talking for this family and its friends. I can work better if I can handle things myself. The half of my job is to save the Sloanes from as many wild rumours as I can."

Wilton nodded approval.

"How about Arthur? You want me to take any questions to him for you?"

"No; thanks.—But," Hastings added, "you might make him see the necessity of telling me what he saw last night. If he doesn't come out with it, he'll make it all the harder on Webster."

"I don't think he saw anything."

"Didn't he? Why'd he refuse to testify before the coroner, then?"

Sheriff Crown's car came whirling up the driveway; and Hastings spoke hurriedly:

"You know he's not as sick as he makes out. He's got to tell me what he knows, judge! He's holding back something. That's why he wants to make me so mad I'll quit the case. Who's he shielding? That's what people will want to know."

Wilton pondered that.

"I'll see what I can do," he finally agreed. "According to you, it may appear—people may suspect—that Webster's guilty or shielding somebody else; and Arthur's guilty or shielding Webster!"

When Mr. Crown reached the porch, they were discussing Webster's condition, and Hastings, with the aid of the judge's penknife, was tightening a screw in his big barlowesque blade. They were careful to say nothing that might arouse the sheriff's suspicion of their compact—an agreement whereby a private detective, and not the law's representative, was to have the benefit of all the judge's information bearing on the murder.

Mr. Crown, however, was dissatisfied.

"I'm tied up!" he complained, nursing with forefinger and thumb his knuckle-like chin. "The only place I can get information is at the wrong end—Russell!"

"What's the matter with me?" the detective asked amiably. "I'll be glad to help—if you think I can."

"What good's that to me?" He wore his best politician's smile, but there was resentment in his voice. "Your job is keeping things quiet—for Sloanehurst. Mr. Sloane's ill, too ill to see me without endangering his life, so his funeral-faced valet tells me. Miss Lucille says, politely enough, she's told all she knows, told it on the stand, and I'm to go to you if I want anything more from her. The judge here knows nothing about the inside relationships of the family and Webster, or of Webster and the Brace girl. And Webster's down and out, thoroughly and conveniently! If all that don't catch your uncle Robert where the hair's short, I'll quit!"

"What do you want to know?" Hastings countered. "You've had access to everything, far as I can see."

Reply to that was delayed by the appearance of Jarvis, summoning the judge to Arthur Sloane's room.

"I want to get at Webster," Crown told Hastings. "And here's why: if Russell didn't kill her, Webster did."

"Why, you've weakened!" the old man guyed head bent over his whittling. "You had Russell's goose cooked this morning—roasted to a rich, dark brown!"

"Yes; and if I could break down his alibi, I'd still have him cooked!"

"You accept the alibi, then?"

"Sure, I accept it."

"I don't."

"Why don't you?" objected Crown. "He didn't have an aeroplane in his hip pocket, did he? That's the only way he could have covered those four miles in fifteen minutes.—Or does his alibi have to fall in order to save Miss Sloane's fiancé?"

He slapped his thigh and thrust out his bristly moustache. "You're paid to fasten the thing on Russell," he said, clearly pugnacious. "I don't expect you to help me work against Webster! I'm not that simple!"

The old man, with a gesture no more arresting than to point at the sheriff with the piece of wood in his left hand, made the official jaw drop almost to the official chest.

"Mr. Crown," he said, "get this, once and for all: a man ain't necessarily a crook because he's once worked for the government. I'm as anxious to find the guilty man now, every time, as when I was in the Department of Justice. And I intend to. From now on, you'll give me credit for that!— Won't you, Mr. Sheriff?"

Crown apologized. "I'm worried; that's what. I'm up a gum stump and can't get down."

"All right, but don't try to make a ladder out of me! Why don't you look into that alibi?"

Crown was irritated again. "What do you stick to that for?"

"Because," Hastings declared, "I'm ready to swear-and-cross-my-heart he lied when he said he ran that four miles. I'm ready to swear he was here when the murder was done. When a man's got as good an alibi as he said he had, his adam's-apple don't play 'Yankee Doodle' on his windpipe."

"Is that so!"

"It is—and here's another thing: when's Mrs. Brace going to break loose?"

"Now, you're talking!" agreed Crown, with momentary enthusiasm. "She told me this morning she'd help me show up Webster—she wouldn't have it that Russell killed the girl. Foxy business! Mixed up in it herself, she runs to the rescue of the man she—"

The sheriff paused, unable to bring that reasoning to its logical conclusion.

"No," he said, dejected; "I can't believe she put him up to murdering her daughter."

"That woman," Hastings said, "is capable of anything—anything! We're going to find she's terrible, I tell you, Crown. She's mixed up in the murder somehow—and, if you don't find out how, I will!"

"How can we get her?" Crown argued. "She was in her flat when the killing was done. We've searched these grounds, and found nothing to incriminate anybody. All we've got is a strong suspicion against two men. She's out and away."

"Not if we watch her. She's promised to make trouble—she'll be lucky if she makes none for herself. Let's keep after her."

"I'm on! But," the sheriff reminded, again half-hearted, "that won't get us anything soon. She won't leave her flat before the funeral."

"That won't keep her quiet very long," Hastings contended. "She told me the funeral would be at nine o'clock tomorrow morning—from an undertaker's.—Anyway, I've instructed one of my assistants to keep track of her. I'm not counting on her grief absorbing her, even for today."

But he saw that Crown was not greatly impressed with the possibility of finding the murderer through Mrs. Brace. The sheriff was engrossed in mental precautions against being misled by "the Sloanehurst detective."

He was still in that mood when Miss Sloane sent for Hastings.

The detective found her in the music room. She had taken the chair which Judge Wilton had occupied an hour before, and was leaning one elbow on an arm of it, her chin resting in the cup of her hand. Her dress—a filmy lavender so light that it shaded almost to pink, and magically made to bring out the grace of her figure—drew his attention to the slight sag of her shoulders, suggestive of great weariness.

But he was captivated anew by her grave loveliness, and by her fortitude. She betrayed her agitation only in the fine tremour in her hands and a certain slowness in her words.

On the porch, talking to Judge Wilton, he had wondered, in a moment of irritation, why he continued on the case against so much apparent opposition in the very household which he sought to help. He knew now that neither his sense of duty nor his fee was the deciding influence. He stayed because this girl needed him, because he had seen in her eyes last night the haggard look of an unspeakable suspicion.

"You wanted to see me—is there anything special?" she asked him, immediately alert.

"Yes; there is, Miss Sloane," he said, careful to put into his voice all the sympathy he felt for her.

"Yes?" She was looking at him with steady eyes.

"It's this, and I want you to bear in mind that I wouldn't bring it up but for my desire to put an end to your uncertainty: I'm afraid you haven't told me everything you know, everything you saw last night in—"

When she would have spoken, he put up a warning hand.

"Let me explain, please. Don't commit yourself until you see what I mean. Judge Wilton and Mr. Webster seem to think I'm not needed here. It may be a natural attitude—for them. They're both lawyers, and to lawyers a mere detective doesn't amount to much."

"Oh, I'm sure it isn't that," she flashed out, apologizing.

"Oh, I don't mind, personally," he said, with a smile for which she felt grateful. "As I say, it's natural for them to think that way, perhaps. Your father, however, is not a lawyer; and, when I went into his room at your request, he took pains to offend me, insult me, several times." That brought a faint flush to her face. "So, that leaves only you to give me facts which I must have—if they exist."

He became more urgent.

"And you employed me, Miss Sloane; you appealed to me when you were at a loss where to turn. I'm only fair to myself as well as to you when I tell you that your distress, far more than financial considerations, persuaded me to undertake this work without first consulting your father."

She leaned toward him, bending from the waist, her eyes slightly widened, so that their effect was to give her a startled air.

"You don't mean you'll give it up!" she said, plainly entreating. "You won't give it up!"

"Are you quite sure you don't want me to give it up? Judge Wilton has asked me twice, out of politeness, not to give it up. Are you merely being polite?"

She smiled, looking tired, and shook her head.

"Really, Mr. Hastings, if you were to desert us now, I should be desperate—altogether. Desperate! Just that."

"I can't desert you," he said gently. "As I told Mr. Webster, I know too little and I suspect too much to do that."

Before she spoke again, she looked at him intently, drawing in her under lip a little against her teeth.

"What, Mr. Hastings?" she asked, then. "What do you suspect?"

"Let me answer that with a question," he suggested. "Last night, your one idea was that I could protect you and your father, everybody in the house here, by acting as your spokesman. I think you wanted to set me up as a buffer between all of you on the one side and the authorities and the reporters on the other. You wanted things kept down, nothing to get out beyond that which was unavoidable. Wasn't that it?"

"Yes; it was," she admitted, not seeing where his question led.

"You were afraid, then, that something incriminating might be divulged, weren't you?"

"Oh, no!" she denied instantly.

"I mean something which might seem incriminating. You trusted the person whom it would seem to incriminate; and you wanted time for the murderer to be found without, in the meantime, having the adverse circumstance made public. Isn't that it, Miss Sloane?"

"Yes—practically."

"Let's be clear on that. Your fear was that too much questioning of you or the other person might result in a slip-up—might make you or him mention the apparently damaging incident, with disastrous effect. Wasn't that it?"

"Yes; that was it."

"Now, what was that apparently incriminating incident?"

She started. He had brought her so directly to the confession that she saw now the impossibility of withholding what he sought.

"It may be," he tried to lighten her responsibility, "the very thing that Webster and the judge have concealed—for I'm sure they're keeping something back. Perhaps, if I knew it, things would be easier. People closely affected by a crime are the last to judge such things accurately."

She gave a long breath of relief, looking at him with perplexity never-theless.

"Yes—I know. That was why I came to you—last night—in the begin-ning."

"And it was about them, Webster and Wilton," he drew the conclusion for her, still encouraging her with his smile, regarding her over the rims of his spectacles with a fatherly kindness.

She turned from him and looked out of the window. It was the middle of a hot, still day, no breeze stirring, and wonderfully quiet. For the mo-ment, there was no sound, in the house or outside.

"Oh!" she cried, her voice a revelation of the extent to which her doubts had oppressed her. "It was like that, out there—quiet, still! If you could only understand!"

"My dear child," he said, "rely on me. The sheriff is bound to assert himself, to keep in the front of things; he's that kind of a man. He'll make an arrest any time, or announce that he will. Don't you see the danger?" He leaned forward and took her hand, a move to which she seemed oblivious. "Don't you see I must have facts to go on—if I'm to help you?"

At that, she disengaged her hand, and sat very straight, her face again a little turned from him. A twitch, like a shudder cut short, moved her whole body, so that the heel of her slipper rapped smartly on the floor.

"I wish," she whispered dully, "I wish I knew what to do!"

"Tell me," he urged, as if he spoke to a child.

She showed him her face, very white, with sudden shadows under the eyes.

"I must, I think; I must tell you," she said, not much louder than the previous whisper. "You were right. I didn't tell the whole story of what I saw. Believe me, I didn't think it mattered. I thought, really, things would right themselves and explanations be unnecessary. But you knew—didn't you?"

"Yes. I knew." He realized her ordeal, helping her through it. "What were they doing?"

She held her chin high.

"It was all true, what I told you in the library, my being waked up by father's moving about, my going to the window, my seeing Berne and the judge facing each other across—her—there at the end of the awful yellow arm of light. But that wasn't all. The moment the light flashed on, the judge threw back his head a little, like a man about to cry out, shout for help. I am sure that was it.

"But Berne was too quick for that. Berne put out his hand; his arm shot across her; and his hand closed the judge's mouth. The judge made no noise whatever, but he shook his head from side to side two or three times—I'm not certain how many—while Berne leant over the body and whispered to him. It seemed to me I could almost hear the words, but I didn't.

"Then Berne took his hand from the judge's mouth. I think, before that, the judge made a sign, tried to nod his head up and down, to show he would do as Berne said. Then, when they saw she was dead, they both hurried around the corner to the front of the house, and I heard them come in; I heard the judge call to father and run up to your room."

She was alarmed then by the amazement and disapproval in his face.

"Oh!" she said, and this time she took his hand. "You see! You see! You don't understand! You think Berne killed her!"

"I don't know," he said, wondering. "I must think." For the moment, indignation swept him. "Wilton! A judge, a judge!—keeping quiet on a thing like that! I must think."

XI

Motives Revealed

She let go his hand and, still leaning toward him, waited for him to speak. A confusion of misgivings assailed her—she regretted having confided in him. If his anger embraced Berne as well as Judge Wilton, she had done nothing but harm!

Seeing her dismay, he tried again to reassure her.

"But no matter!" he minimized his own sense of shock. "I'm sure I'll understand if you'll tell me more—your explanation."

Obviously, the only inference he could draw from her story as she had told it was that Webster had killed the woman and, found bending over her body, had sprung forward to silence the man who had discovered him. Nevertheless, it was equally evident that she was sincere in attributing to Webster a different motive for preventing the judge's outcry. Consideration of that persuaded Hastings that she could give him facts which would change the whole aspect of the crime.

Her hesitance now made him uneasy; he recognized the necessity of increasing her reliance upon him. If she told him only a part of what she knew, he would be scarcely in a better position than before.

"Naturally," he added, "you can throw light on the whole incident—light by which I must be guided, to a great degree."

"If Berne were not ill," she responded to that, "I wouldn't tell.—It's because he's lying up there, his lips closed, unable to keep a look-out for developments, at the mercy of what the sheriff may do or say!—That's why I feel so dreadfully the need of help, Mr. Hastings!"

She slid back in her chair, moving farther from him, as if his kindly gaze disconcerted her.

"If he hadn't suffered this collapse, I should have left the matter to him, I think. But now—now I can't!" She straightened again, her chin up, the signal with her of final decision. "He acted on his impulsive desire to prevent my being shocked by that discovery—that horror out there on the lawn. Things had happened to convince him that such a thing, shouted through the night, would be a terrific blow to me. I'm sure that that was the only idea he had when he put his hand over Judge Wilton's mouth."

"I can believe that," he said. "Tell me why you believe it."

"Oh!" she protested, hands clenched on her knees; "if it affected only him and me!"

Her suspicion of her father recurred to him. It was, he thought, back of the terror he saw in her eyes now.

"But it does affect only him and me, after all!" she continued fiercely, as much to strengthen herself in what she wanted to believe as to force him to that belief. "Let me tell you the whole affair, from beginning to end."

She proceeded in a low tone, the words slower, as if she laboured for precision and clarity.

"I must go back to Friday—the night before last—it seems months ago! I had heard that Berne had become involved in some sort of relationship with his stenographer—that she had been dismissed from his office and refused to accept the dismissal as final. I mean, of course, I heard she was in love with him, and he'd been in love with her—or should have been.

"It was told me by a friend of mine in Washington, Lucy Carnly. It seems another stenographer overheard the conversation between Berne and Miss—Miss Brace. It got out that way. It was very circumstantial; I couldn't help believing it, some of it; Lucy wouldn't have brought me idle gossip—I thought."

She drew in her under lip, to hide its momentary tremour, and shook her head from side to side once.

"All that, Mr. Hastings, came up, as a matter of course, when Berne reached here evening before last for the week-end. I'd just heard it that day. He denied it, said there had been nothing remotely resembling a love af-fair.—He was indignant, and very hurt!—He said she'd misconstrued some of his kindnesses to her. He couldn't explain how she had misconstrued them. At any rate, the result was that I broke our engagement. I—"

"Friday night!" Hastings exclaimed involuntarily.

He grasped on the instant how grossly Webster, by withholding all this, had deceived him, left him in the dark.

"Yes; and I told father about it," she hurried her words here, the effect of her manner being the impression that she hoped this fact would not bulk too large in the detective's thoughts. "The three of us had a talk about it Friday night. Father's wonderfully fond of Berne and tried to persuade me I was foolishly ruining my life. I refused to change my mind. When I went upstairs, they stayed a long time in the library, talking.

"I think they decided the best thing for Berne was to stay on here, through yesterday and today, in the hope that he and father might change my mind. Father tried to, yesterday morning. He was awfully upset. That's one reason he's so worn out and sick today.—I love my father so, Mr. Hast-ings!" She held her lips tight-shut a moment, a sob struggling in her throat. "But my distress, my own hurt pride—"

"What did your father say about Mildred Brace?" Hastings asked, when she did not finish that sentence.

She looked at him, again with widened eyes, a startled air, putting both her hands to her throat.

"There!" she said, voice falling to a whisper.

Then, turning her face half from him, she whispered so low that he heard her with difficulty: "I wish I were dead!"

Her words frightened him, they had so clearly the ring of truth, as if she would in sober fact have preferred death to the thought which was breaking her heart—suspicion of her father.

"That was why Berne stopped the judge's outcry," she said at last, turning her white face to him; "he had the sudden wild idea that I'm afraid you have—that father might have killed her. And Berne did not want that awful fact screamed through the night at me. Oh, can't you see—can't you see that, Mr. Hastings?"

"It's entirely possible; Mr. Webster may have thought that.—But let's keep the story straight. What had your father said about Mildred Brace—to arouse any such suspicion?"

"He was angry, terribly indignant. You know I made no secret to you of his high temper. His rages are fierce.—Once, when he was that way, I saw him kill a dog. If it had—but I think all men who're unstrung nervously, as he is, have high tempers. He felt so indignant because she had come between Berne and myself. He blamed neither Berne nor me. He seemed to concentrate all his anger upon her.

"He said—you see, Mr. Hastings, I tell you everything!—he threatened to go to her and— He had, of course, no definite idea what he would do. Finally, he did say he would buy her off, pay her to leave this part of the country. After that, he said, he knew I would 'see things clearly,' and Berne and I would be reconciled."

Hastings remembered Russell's assertion that Mildred had her ticket to Chicago.

"Did he buy her off?" he asked quickly.

"Oh, no; he was merely wishing that he could, I think."

"But he made no attempt to get in touch with her yesterday? You're sure?"

"Quite," she said. "But don't you see. Mr. Hastings? Father was so intense in his hatred of her that Berne thought of him the moment he found that body—out there. He thought father must have encountered her on the lawn in some way, or she must have come after him, and he, in a fit of rage, struck her down."

"Has Webster told you this?"

"No—but it's true; it is!"

"But, if your supposition is to hold good, how did your father happen to be in possession of that dagger, which evidently was made with malice aforethought, as the lawyers say?"

"Exactly," she said, her lips quivering, hands gripping spasmodically at her knees. "He didn't do it! He didn't do it! Berne's idea was a mistake!"

"Who, then?" he pressed her, realizing now that she was so unstrung she would give him her thoughts unguarded.

"Why, that man Russell," she said, her voice so low and the words so slow that he thought her at the limit of her endurance. "But I've said all this to show you why Berne put his hand over the judge's mouth. I want to make it very clear that he feared father—think of it, Mr. Hastings!—had killed her! At first, I thought—"

She bowed her face in both her hands and wept unrestrainedly, without sobs, the tears streaming between her fingers and down her wrists.

The old man put one hand on her hair, and with the other brought forth his handkerchief, being bothered by the sudden mistiness of his spectacles.

"A brave girl," he said, his own voice insecure. "What a woman! I know what you mean. At first, you feared your father might have been concerned in the murder. I saw it in your eyes last night. You had the same thought that young Webster had—rather, that you say he had."

Her weeping ceased as suddenly as it had begun. She looked at him through tears.

"And I've only injured Berne in your eyes; I think, irreparably! This morning I thought you heard me when I asked him not to let it be known that our engagement was broken? Don't you remember? You were on the porch as we came around the corner."

For the first time since its utterance, he recalled her statement then, "We'll have to leave it as it was," and Webster's significant rejoinder. He despised his own stupidity. Had he magnified Webster's desire to keep that promise into guilty knowledge of the crime itself? And had not the mistake driven him into false and valueless interpretations of his entire interview with Webster?

"He promised," Lucille pursued, "for the same reason I had in asking it—to prevent discovery of the fact that father might have had a motive for wishing her dead! It was a mistake, I see now, a terrible mistake!"

"Can you tell me why you didn't have the same thoughts about Berne?" He was sorry he had to make that inquiry. If he could, he would have spared her further distress. "Why wouldn't he have had the same motive, hatred of Mildred Brace, a thousand times stronger?"

"I don't know," she said. "I simply never thought of it—not once."

Fine psychologist that he was, Hastings knew why that view had not occurred to her. Her love for Webster was an idealizing sentiment, putting him beyond even the possibility of wrong-doing. Her love for her father, unusual in its devotion as it was, recognized his weaknesses nevertheless.

And, while seeking to protect the two, she had told a story which, so far as bald facts went, incriminated the lover far more than the father. She had attributed to Sloane, in her uneasiness, the motive which would have been most natural to the discarded Webster. Even now, she could not suspect Berne; her only fear was that others, not understanding him as she did, might suspect him! Although she had broken with him, she still loved him. More than that: his illness and consequent helplessness increased her devotion for him, brought to the surface the maternal phase of it.

"If she had to choose between the two," Hastings thought, "she'd save Webster—every time!"

"I know—I tell you, Mr. Hastings, I *know* neither Berne nor father is at all responsible for this crime. I tell you," she repeated, rising to her feet, as if by mere physical height she hoped to impress her knowledge upon him, "I *know* they're innocent.—Don't *you* know it?"

She stood looking down at him, her whole body tense, arms held close against her sides, the knuckles of her fingers white as ivory. Her eyes now were dry, and brilliant.

He evaded the flat statement to which she pressed him.

"But your knowledge, Miss Sloane, and what we must prove," he said, also standing, "are two different things just now. The authorities will demand proofs."

"I know. That's why I've told you these things." Somehow, her manner reproached him. "You said you had to have them in order to handle this—this situation properly. Now that you know them, I'm sure you'll feel safe in devoting all your time to proving Russell's guilt." She moved her head forward, to study him more closely. "You know he's guilty, don't you?"

"I'm certain Mrs. Brace figured in her daughter's murder," he said. "She was concerned in it somehow. If that's true, and if your father approached neither her nor her daughter yesterday, it does seem highly possible that Russell's guilty."

He turned from her and stood at the window, his back to her a few long moments. When he faced her again, he looked old.

"But the facts—if we could only break down Russell's alibi!"

"Oh!" she whispered, in new alarm. "I'd forgotten that!"

All the tenseness went out of her limbs. She sank into her chair, and sat there, looking up to him, her eyes frankly confessing a panic fear.

"I think I'm sorry I told you," she said, desperately. "I can't make you understand!" Another consideration forced itself upon her. "You won't have to tell anybody—anybody at all—about this, will you—now?"

He was prepared for that.

"I'll have to ask Judge Wilton why he acted on Mr. Webster's advice—and what that advice was, what they whispered to each other when you saw them."

"Why, that's perfectly fair," she assented, relieved. "That will stop all the secrecy between them and me. It's the very thing I want. If that's assured, everything else will work itself out."

Her faith surprised him. He had not realized how unqualified it was.

"Did you ask the judge about it?" he inquired.

"Yes; just before I came in here—after Berne's collapse. I felt so helpless! But he tried to persuade me my imagination had deceived me; he said they had had no such scene. You know how gruff and hard Judge Wilton can be at times. I shouldn't choose him for a confidant."

"No; I reckon not. But we'll ask him now—if you don't mind."

Willis, the butler, answered the bell, and gave information: Judge Wilton had left Sloanehurst half an hour ago and had gone to the Randalls'. He had asked for Miss Sloane, but, learning that she was engaged, had left his regrets, saying he would come in tomorrow, after the adjournment of court.

"He's on the bench tomorrow at the county-seat," Lucille explained the message. "He always divides his time between us and the Randalls when he comes down from Fairfax for his court terms. He told me this morning he'd come back to us later in the week."

"On second thought," Hastings said, "that's better. I'll talk to him alone tomorrow—about this thing, this inexplicable thing: a judge taking it upon himself to deceive the sheriff even! But," he softened the sternness of his tone, "he must have a reason, a better one than I can think of now." He smiled. "And I'll report to you, when he's told me."

"I'm glad it's tomorrow," she said wearily. "I—I'm tired out."

On his way back to Washington, the old man reflected: "Now, she'll persuade Sloane to do the sensible thing—talk." Then, to bolster that hope, he added a stern truth: "He's got to. He can't gag himself with a pretended illness forever!"

At the same time the girl he had left in the music room wept again, saying over and over to herself, in a despair of doubt: "Not that! Not that! I couldn't tell him that. I told him enough. I know I did. He wouldn't have understood!"

XII

Hendricks Reports

In his book-lined, "loosely furnished" apartment Sunday afternoon Hastings whittled prodigiously, staring frequently at the flap of the grey envelope with the intensity of a crystal-gazer. Once or twice he pronounced aloud possible meanings of the symbols imprinted on the scrap of paper.

"'—edly de—,'" he worried. "That might stand for 'repeatedly demanded' or 'repeatedly denied' or 'undoubtedly denoted' or a hundred— But that 'Pursuit!' is the core of the trouble. They put the pursuit on him, sure as you're knee-high to a hope of heaven!"

The belief grew in him that out of those pieces of words would come solution of his problem. The idea was born of his remarkable instinct. Its positiveness partook of superstition—almost. He could not shake it off. Once he chuckled, appreciating the apparent absurdity of trying to guess the criminal meaning, the criminal intent, back of that writing. But he kept to his conjecturing.

He had many interruptions. Newspaper reporters, instantly impressed by the dramatic possibilities, the inherent sensationalism, of the murder, flocked to him. Referred to him by the people at Sloanehurst, they asked for not only his narration of what had occurred but also for his opinion as to the probability of running down the guilty man.

He would make no predictions, he told them, confining himself to a simple statement of facts. When one young sleuth suggested that both Sloane and Webster feared arrest on the charge of murder and had relied on his reputation to prevent prompt action against them by the sheriff, the old man laughed. He knew the futility of trying to prevent publication of intimations of that sort.

But he took advantage of the opportunity to put a different interpretation on his employment by the Sloanes.

"Seems to me," he contributed, "it's more logical to say that their calling in a detective goes a long way to show their innocence of all connection with the crime. They wouldn't pay out real money to have themselves hunted, if they were guilty, would they?"

Afterwards, he was glad he had emphasized this point. In the light of subsequent events, it looked like actual foresight of Mrs. Brace's tactics.

Soon after five Hendricks came in, to report. He was a young man, stockily built, with eyes that were always on the verge of laughter and lips that sloped inward as if biting down on the threatened mirth. The shape of his lips was symbolical of his habit of discourse; he was of few words.

"Webster," he said, standing across the table from his employer and shooting out his words like a memorized speech, "been overplaying his hand financially. That's the rumour; nothing tangible yet. Gone into real estate and building projects; associated with a crowd that has the name of operating on a shoestring. Nobody'd be surprised if they all blew up."

"As a real-estate man, I take it," Hastings commented, slowly shaving off thin slivers of chips from his piece of pine, "he's a brilliant young lawyer. That's it?"

"Yes, sir," Hendricks agreed, the slope of his lips accentuated.

"Keep after that, tomorrow.—What about Mrs. Brace?"

"Destitute, practically; in debt; threatened with eviction; no resources."

"So money, lack of it, is bothering her as well as Webster!—How much is she in debt?"

"Enough to be denied all credit by the stores; between five and seven hundred, I should say. That's about the top mark for that class of trade."

"All right, Hendricks; thanks," the old man commended warmly. "That's great work, for Sunday.—Now, Russell's room?"

"Yes, sir; I went over it."

"Find any steel on the floor?"

Hendricks took from his pocket a little paper parcel about the size of a man's thumb.

"Not sure, sir. Here's what I got."

He unfolded the paper and put it down on the table, displaying a small mass of what looked like dust and lint.

"Wonderful what a magnet will pick up, ain't it?" mused his employer: "I got the same sort of stuff at Sloanehurst this morning.—I'll go over this, look for the steel particles, right away."

"Anything else, sir—special?"

The assistant was already half-way to the door. He knew that a floor an inch deep in chips from his employer's whittling indicated laborious mental gropings by the old man. It was no time for superfluous words.

"After dinner," Hastings instructed, "relieve Gore—at the Walman. Thanks."

As Hendricks went out, there was another telephone call, this time from Crown, to make amends for coolness he had shown Hastings at Sloanehurst.

"I was wrong, and you were right," he conceded, handsomely; "I mean about that Brace woman. Better keep your man on her trail."

"What's up?" Hastings asked amicably.

"That's what I want to know! I've seen her again. I couldn't get anything more from her except threats. She's going on the warpath. She told me: 'Tomorrow I'll look into things for myself. I'll not sit here idle and leave everything to a sheriff who wants campaign contributions and a detective who's paid to hush things up!' You can see her saying that, can't you? Wow!"

"That all?"

"That's all, right now. But I've got a suspicion she knows more than we think. When she makes up her mind to talk, she'll say something!—Mr. Hastings," Crown added, as if he imparted a tremendous fact, "that woman's smart! I tell you, she's got brains, a head full of 'em!"

"So I judged," the detective agreed, drily. "By the way, have you seen Russell again?"

"Yes. There's another thing. I don't see where you get that stuff about his weak alibi. It's copper-riveted!"

"He says so, you mean."

"Yes; and the way he says it. But I followed your advice. I've advertised, through the police here and up and down the Atlantic coast, for any automobile party or parties who went along that Sloanehurst road last night between ten-thirty and eleven-thirty."

"Fine!" Hastings congratulated. "But get me straight on that: I don't say any of them saw him; I say there's a chance that he was seen."

The old man went back, not to examination of Hendricks' parcel, but to further consideration of the possible contents of the letter that had been in the grey envelope. Russell, he reflected, had been present when Mildred Brace mailed it, and, what was more important, when Mildred started out of the apartment with it.

He made sudden decision: he would question Russell again. Carefully placing Hendricks' package of dust and lint in a drawer of the table, he set out for the Eleventh street boarding house.

It was, however, not Russell who figured most prominently in the accounts of the murder published by the Monday morning newspapers. The reporters, resenting the reticence they had encountered at Sloanehurst, and making much of Mrs. Brace's threats, put in the forefront of their stories an appealing picture of a bereaved mother's one-sided fight for justice against the baffling combination of the Sloanehurst secretiveness and indifference and the mysterious circumstances of the daughter's death. Not one of them questioned the validity of Russell's alibi.

"With the innocence of the dead girl's fiancé established," said one account, "Sheriff Crown last night made no secret of his chagrin that Berne Webster had collapsed at the very moment when the sheriff was on the point of putting him through a rigid cross-examination. The young lawyer's retirement from the scene, coupled with the Sloane family's retaining the celebrated detective, Jefferson Hastings, as a buffer against any questioning of the Sloanehurst people, has given Society, here and in Virginia, a topic for discussion of more than ordinary interest."

Another paragraph that caught Hastings' attention, as he read between mouthfuls of his breakfast, was this:

"Mrs. Brace, discussing the tragedy with a reporter last night, showed a surprising knowledge of all its incidents. Although she had not left her apartment in the Walman all day, she had been questioned by both Sheriff Crown and Mr. Hastings, not to mention the unusually large number of newspaper writers who besieged her for interviews.

"And it seemed that, in addition to answering the queries put to her by the investigators, she had accomplished a vast amount of keen inquiry on her own account. When talking to her, it is impossible for one to escape the impression that this extraordinarily intelligent woman believes she can prove the guilt of the man who struck down her daughter."

"Just what I was afraid of," thought the detective. "Nearly every paper siding with her!"

His face brightened.

"All the better," he consoled himself. "More chance of her overreaching herself—as long as she don't know what I suspect. I'll get the meaning of that grey letter yet!"

But he was worried. Berne Webster's collapse, he knew, was too convenient for Webster—it looked like pretence. Ninety-nine out of every hundred newspaper readers would consider his illness a fake, the obvious trick to escape the work of explaining what seemed to be inexplicable circumstances.

To Hastings the situation was particularly annoying because he had brought it about; his own questioning had turned out to be the straw that broke the suspected man's endurance.

"Always blundering!" he upbraided himself. "Trying to be so all-shot smart, I overplayed my hand."

He got Dr. Garnet on the wire.

"Doctor," he said, in a tone that implored, "I'm obliged to see Webster today."

"Sorry, Mr. Hastings," came the instant refusal; "but it can't be done."

"For one question," qualified Hastings; "less than a minute's talk—one word, 'yes' or 'no'? It's almost a matter of life and death."

"If that man's excited about anything," Garnet retorted, "it will be entirely a matter of death. Frankly, I couldn't see my way clear to letting you question him if his escaping arrest depended on it. I called in Dr. Welles last night; and I'm giving you his opinion as well as my own."

"When can I see him, then?"

"I can't answer that. It may be a week; it may be a month. All I can tell you today is that you can't question him now."

With that information, Hastings decided to interview Judge Wilton.

"He's the next best," he thought. "That whispering across the woman's body—it's got to be explained, and explained right!"

As a matter of fact, he had refrained from this inquiry the day before, so that his mind might not be clouded by anger. His deception by the judge had greatly provoked him.

XIII

Mrs. Brace Begins

Court had recessed for lunch when Hastings, going down a second-story corridor of the Alexandria county courthouse, entered Judge Wilton's anteroom. His hand was raised to knock on the door of the inner office when he heard the murmur of voices on the other side. He took off his hat and sat down, welcoming the breeze that swept through the room, a refreshing contrast to the forenoon's heat and smother downstairs.

He reached for his knife and piece of pine, checked the motion and glanced swiftly toward the closed door. A high note of a woman's voice touched his memory, for a moment confusing him. But it was for a moment only. While the sound was still in his ears, he remembered where he had heard it before—from Mrs. Brace when, toward the close of his interview with her, she had shrilly denounced Berne Webster.

Mrs. Brace, her daughter's funeral barely three hours old, had started to make her threats good.

While he was considering that, the door of the private office swung inward, Judge Wilton's hand on the knob. It opened on the middle of a sentence spoken by Mrs. Brace:

"—tell you, you're a fool if you think you can put me off with that!"

Her gleaming eyes were so furtive and so quick that they traversed the whole of Wilton's countenance many times, a fiery probe of each separate feature. The inflections of her voice invested her words with ugliness; but she did not shriek.

"You bully everybody else, but not me! They don't call you 'Hard Tom Wilton' for nothing, do they? I know you! I know you, I tell you! I was down there in the courtroom when you sentenced that man! You had cruelty in your mind, cruelty on your face. Ugh! And you're cruel to me—and taking an ungodly pleasure in it! Well, let me tell you, I won't be broken by it. I want fair dealing, and I'll have it!"

At that moment, facing full toward Hastings, she caught sight of him. But his presence seemed a matter of no importance to her; it did not break the stream of her fierce invective. She did not even pause.

He saw at once that her anger of yesterday was as nothing to the storming rage which shook her now. Every line of her face revealed malignity.

The eyebrows were drawn higher on her forehead, nearer to the wave of white hair that showed under her black hat. The nostrils dilated and contracted with indescribable rapidity. The lips, thickened and rolling back at intervals from her teeth, revealed more distinctly that animal, exaggerated wetness which had so repelled him.

"You were out there on that lawn!" she pursued, her glance flashing back to the judge. "You were out there when she was killed! If you try to tell me you—"

"Stop it! Stop it!" Wilton commanded, and, as he did so, turned his head to an angle that put Hastings within his field of vision.

The judge, with one hand on the doorknob, had been pressing with the other against the woman's shoulders, trying to thrust her out of the room—a move which she resisted by a hanging-back posture that threw her weight on his arm. He put more strength now into his effort and succeeded in forcing her clear of the threshold. His eyes were blazing under the shadow of his heavy, overhanging brows; but there was about him no suggestion of a loss of self-control.

"I'm glad to see you!" he told Hastings, speaking over Mrs. Brace's head, and smiling a deprecatory recognition of the hopelessness of contending with an infuriated woman.

She addressed them both.

"Smile all you please, now!" she threatened. "But the accounts aren't balanced yet! Wait for what I choose to tell—what I intend to do!"

Suddenly she got herself in hand. It was as unexpected and thorough a transformation as the one Hastings had seen twenty-four hours before during her declaration of Webster's guilt. She had the same appearance now as then, the same tautness of body, the same flat, constrained tone.

She turned to Wilton:

"I ask you again, will you help me as I asked you? Are you going to deny me fair play?"

He looked at her in amazement, scowling.

"What fair play?" he exclaimed, and, without waiting for her reply, said to Hastings: "She insists that I know young Webster killed her daughter, that I can produce the evidence to prove it. Can you disabuse her mind?"

She surprised them by going, slowly and with apparent composure, toward the corridor door. There she paused, looking at first one and then the other with an evil smile so openly contemptuous that it affected them strongly. There was something in it that made it flagrantly insulting. Hastings turned away from her. Judge Wilton gave her look for look, but his already flushed face coloured more darkly.

"Very well, Judge Wilton!" she gave him insolent good-bye, in which there was also unmistakable threat. "You'll do the right thing sooner or later—and as I tell you. You're—get this straight—you're not through with me yet!"

She laughed, one low note, and, impossible as it seemed, proclaimed with the harsh sound an absolute confidence in what she said.

"Nor you, Mr. Hastings!" she continued, taking her time with her words, and waiting until the detective faced her again, before she concluded: "You'll sing a different tune when you find I've got this affair in my hands—tight!"

Still smiling her contempt, as if she enjoyed a feeling of superiority, she left the room. When her footsteps died down the corridor, the two men drew long breaths of relief.

Wilton broke the ensuing silence.

"Is she sane?"

"Yes," Hastings said, "so far as sanity can be said to exist in a mind consecrated to evil."

The judge was surprised by the solemnity of the other's manner. "Why do you say that?" he asked. "Do you know that much about her?"

"Who wouldn't?" Hastings retorted. "It's written all over her."

Wilton led the way into his private office and closed the door.

"I'm glad it happened at just this time," he said, "when everybody's out of the building." He struck the desk with his fist. "By God!" he ground out through gritted teeth. "How I hate these wild, unbridled women!"

"Yes," agreed Hastings, taking the chair Wilton rolled forward for him. "She worries me. Wonder if she's going to Sloanehurst."

"That would be the logical sequel to this visit," Wilton said. "But pardon my show of temper. You came to see me?"

"Yes; and, like her, for information. But," the detective said, smiling, "not for rough-house purposes."

The judge had not entirely regained his equanimity; his face still wore a heightened colour; his whole bearing was that of a man mentally reviewing the results of an unpleasant incident. Instead of replying promptly to Hastings, he sat looking out of the window, obviously troubled.

"Her game is blackmail," he declared at last.

"On whom?" the detective queried.

"Arthur Sloane, of course. She calculates that he'll play to have her cease annoying his daughter's fiancé. And she'll impress Arthur, if Jarvis ever lets her get to him. Somehow, she strangely compels credence."

"Not for me," Hastings objected, and did not point out that Wilton's words might be taken as an admission of Webster's guilt.

The judge himself might have seen that.

"I mean," he qualified, "she seems too smart a woman to put herself in a position where ridicule will be sure to overtake her. And yet, that's what she's doing—isn't she?"

The detective was whittling, dropping the chips into the waste-basket. He spoke with a deliberateness unusual even in him, framing each sentence in his mind before giving it utterance.

"I reckon, judge, you and I have had some four or five talks—that is, not counting Saturday evening and yesterday at Sloanehurst. That's about the extent of our acquaintance. That right?"

"Why, yes," Wilton said, surprised by the change of topic.

"I mention it," Hastings explained, "to show how I've felt toward you—you interested me. Excuse me if I speak plainly—you'll see why later on—but you struck me as worth studying, deep. And I thought you must have sized me up, catalogued me one way or the other. You're like me: waste no time with men who bore you. I felt certain, if you'd been asked, you'd have checked me off as reliable. Would you?"

"Unquestionably."

"And, if I was reliable then, I'm reliable now. That's a fair assumption, ain't it?"

"Certainly." The judge laughed shortly, a little embarrassed.

"That brings me to my point. You'll believe me when I tell you my only interest in this murder is to find the murderer, and, while I'm doing it, to save the Sloanes as much as possible from annoyance. You'll believe me, also, when I say I've got to have all the facts if I'm to work surely and fast. You recognize the force of that, don't you?"

"Why, yes, Hastings." Wilton spoke impatiently this time.

"Fine!" The old man shot him a genial glance over the steel-rimmed spectacles. "That's the introduction. Here's the real thing: I've an idea you could tell me more about what happened on the lawn Saturday night."

After his involuntary, immediate start of surprise, Wilton tilted his head, slowly blowing the cigar smoke from his pursed lips. He had a fine air of reflection, careful thought.

"I can elaborate what I've already told you," he said, finally, "if that's what you mean—go into greater detail."

He watched closely the edge of the detective's face unhidden by his bending over the wood he was cutting.

"I don't think elaboration could do much good," Hastings objected. "I referred to new stuff—some fact or facts you might have omitted, unconsciously."

"Unconsciously?" Wilton echoed the word, as a man does when his mind is overtaxed.

Hastings took it up.

"Or consciously, even," he said quickly, meeting the other's eyes.

The judge moved sharply, bracing himself against the back of the chair.

"What do you mean by that?"

"Skilled in the law yourself, thoroughly familiar, with the rules of evidence, it's more than possible that you might have reviewed matters and decided that there were things which, if they were known, would do harm instead of good—obscure the truth, perhaps; or hinder the hunt for the guilty man instead of helping it on. That's clear enough, isn't it? You might have thought that?"

The look of sullen resentment in the judge's face was unmistakable.

"Oh, say what you mean!" he retorted warmly. "What you're insinuating is that I've lied!"

"It don't have to be called that."

"Well, then, that I, a judge, sworn to uphold the law and punish crime, have elected to thwart the law and to cheat its officials of the facts they should have. Is that what you mean?"

"I'll be honest with you," Hastings admitted, unmoved by the other's grand manner. "I've wondered about that—whether you thought a judge had a right to do a thing of that sort."

Wilton's hand, clenched on the edge of the desk, shook perceptibly.

"Did you think that, judge?" the detective persisted.

The judge hesitated.

"It's a point I've never gone into," he said finally, with intentional sarcasm.

Hastings snapped his knife-blade shut and thrust the piece of wood into his pocket.

"Let's get away from this beating about the bush," he suggested, voice on a sterner note. "I don't want to irritate you unnecessarily, judge. I came here for information—stuff I'm more than anxious to get. And I go back to that now: won't you tell me anything more about the discovery of the woman's body by the two of you—you and Webster?"

"No; I won't! I've covered the whole thing—several times."

"Is there anything that you haven't told—anything you've decided to suppress?"

Wilton got up from his chair and struck the desk with his fist.

"See here, Hastings! You're getting beside yourself. Representing Miss Sloane doesn't warrant your insulting her friends. Suppose we consider this interview at an end. Some other time, perhaps—"

Hastings also had risen.

"Just a minute, judge!" he interrupted, all at once assuming the authoritative air that had so amazed Wilton the night of the murder. "You're suppressing something—and I know it!"

"That's a lie!" Wilton retorted, the flush deepening to crimson on his face.

"It ain't a lie," Hastings contradicted, holding his self-control. "And you watch yourself! Don't you call me a liar again—not as long as you live! You can't afford the insult."

"Then, don't provoke it. Don't—"

"What did Webster whisper to you, across that corpse?" Hastings demanded, going nearer to Wilton.

"What's this?" Wilton's tone was one of consternation; the words might have been spoken by a man stumbling on an unsuspected horror in a dark room.

They stared at each other for several dragging seconds. The detective waved a hand toward the judge's chair.

"Sit down," he said, resuming his own seat.

There followed another pause, longer than the first. The judge's breathing was laboured, audible. He lowered his eyes and passed his hand across their thick lids. When he looked up again, Hastings commanded him with unwavering, expectant gaze.

"I've made a mistake," Wilton began huskily, and stopped.

"Yes?" Hastings said, unbending. "How?"

"I see it now. It was a matter of no importance, in itself. I've exaggerated it, by my silence, into disproportionate significance." His tone changed to curiosity. "Who told you about—the whispering?"

The detective was implacable, emphasizing his dominance.

"First, what was it?" When Wilton still hesitated, he repeated: "What did Webster say when he put his hand over your mouth—to prevent your outcry?"

The judge threw up his head, as if in sudden resolve to be frank. He spoke more readily, with a clumsy semblance of amiability.

"He said, 'Don't do that! You'll frighten Lucille!' I tried to nod my head, agreeing. But he misunderstood the movement, I think. He thought I meant to shout anyway; he tightened his grip. 'Keep quiet! Will you keep quiet?' he repeated two or three times. When I made my meaning clear, he took his hand away. He explained later what had occurred to him the moment Arthur's light flashed on. He said it came to him before he clearly realized who I was. It—

"I swear, Hastings, I hate to tell you this. It suggests unjust suspicions. Of what value are the wild ideas of a nervous man, all to pieces anyway, when he stumbles on a dead woman in the middle of the night?"

"They were valuable enough," Hastings flicked him, "for you to cover them up—for some reason. What were they?"

Wilton was puzzled by the detective's tone, its abstruse insinuation. But he answered the question.

"He said his first idea, the one that made him think of Lucille, was that

Arthur might have had something to do with the murder."

"Why? Why did he think Sloane had killed Mildred Brace?"

"Because she had been the cause of Lucille's breaking her engagement with Berne—and Arthur knew that. Arthur had been in a rage—"

"All right!" Hastings checked him suddenly, and, getting to his feet, fell to pacing the room, his eyes, always on Wilton. "I'm acquainted with that part of it."

He paid no attention to Wilton's evident surprise at that statement. He had a surprise of his own to deal with: the unexpected similarity of the judge's story with Lucille Sloane's theorizing as to what Webster had whispered across the body in the moment of its discovery. The two statements were identical—a coincidence that defied credulity.

He caught himself doubting Lucille. Had she been theorizing, after all? Or had she relayed to him words that Wilton had put into her mouth? Then, remembering her grief, her desperate appeals to him for aid, he dismissed the suspicion.

"I'd stake my life on her honesty," he decided. "Her intuition gave her the correct solution—if Wilton's not lying now!"

He put the obvious question: "Judge, am I the first one to hear this— from you?" and received the obvious answer: "You are. I didn't volunteer it to you, did I?"

"All right. Now, did you believe Webster? Wait a minute! Did you believe his fear wasn't for himself when he gagged you that way?"

"Yes; I did," replied Wilton, in a tone that lacked sincerity.

"Do you believe it now?"

"If I didn't, do you think I'd have tried for a moment to conceal what he said to me?"

"Why did you conceal it?"

"Because Arthur Sloane was my friend, and his daughter's happiness would have been ruined if I'd thrown further suspicion on him. Besides, what I did conceal could have been of no value to any detective or sheriff on earth. It meant nothing, so long as I knew the boy's sincerity—and his innocence as well as Arthur's."

"But," Hastings persisted, "why all this concern for Webster, after his engagement had been broken?"

"How's that?" Wilton countered. "Oh, I see! The break wasn't permanent. Arthur and I had decided on that. We knew they'd get together again."

Hastings halted in front of the judge's chair.

"Have you kept back anything else?" he demanded.

"Nothing," Wilton said, with a return of his former sullenness. "And," he forced himself to the avowal, "I'm sorry I kept that back. It's nothing."

Hastings' manner changed on the instant. He was once more cordial.

"All right, judge!" he said heartily, consulting his ponderous watch. "This is all between us. I take it, you wouldn't want it known by the sheriff, even now?" Wilton shook his head in quick negation. "All right! He needn't—if things go well. And the person I got it from won't spread it around.—That satisfactory?"

The judge's smile, in spite of his best effort, was devoid of friendliness. The dark flush that persisted in his countenance told how hardly he kept down his anger.

Hastings put on his hat and ambled toward the door.

"By the way," he proclaimed an afterthought, "I've got to ask one more favour, judge. If Mrs. Brace troubles you again, will you let me know about it, at the earliest possible moment?"

He went out, chuckling.

But the judge was as mystified as he was resentful. He had detected in Hastings' manner, he thought, the same self-satisfaction, the same quiet elation, which he and Berne had observed at the close of the music-room interview. Going to the window, he addressed the summer sky:

"Who the devil does the old fool suspect—Arthur or Berne?"

XIV

Mr. Crown Forms an Alliance

"If you've as much as five hundred dollars at your disposal—pin-money savings, perhaps—anything you can check on without the knowledge of others, you can do it," Hastings urged, ending a long argument.

"I! Take it to her myself?" Lucille still protested, although she could not refute his reasonings.

"It's the only way that would be effective—and it wouldn't be so difficult. I had counted on your courage—your unusual courage."

"But what will it accomplish? If I could only see that, clearly!"

She was beginning to yield to his insistence.

They were in the rose garden, in the shade of a little arbor from whose roof the great red flowers drooped almost to the girl's hair. He was acutely aware of the pathetic contrast between her white, ravaged face and the surrounding scene, the fragrance, the roses of every colour swaying to the slow breeze of late afternoon, the long, cool shadows. He found it hard to force her to the plan, and would have abandoned it but for the possibilities it presented to his mind.

"I've already touched on that," he applied himself to her doubts. "I want you to trust me there, to accept my solemn assurance that, if Mrs. Brace accepts this money from you on our terms, it will hasten my capture of the murderer. I'll say more than that: you are my only possible help in the matter. Won't you believe me?"

She sat quite still, a long time, looking steadily at him with unseeing eyes.

"I shall have to go to that dreadful woman's apartment, be alone with her, make a secret bargain," she enumerated the various parts of her task, wonder and repugnance mingling in her voice. "That horrible woman! You say, yourself, Mr. Hastings, she's horrible."

"Still," he repeated, "you can do it."

A little while ago she had cried out, both hands clenched on the arm of the rustic bench, her eyes opening wide in the startled look he had come to know: "If I could do something, *anything*, for Berne! Dr. Welles said only an hour ago he had no more than an even chance for his life. Half the time he can't speak! And I'm responsible. I am! I know it. I try to think I'm not.

But I am!"

He recurred to that.

"Dr. Welles said the ending of Mr. Webster's suspense would be the best medicine for him. And I think Webster would see that nobody but you could do this—in the very nature of things. The absolute secrecy required, the fact that you buy her silence, pay her to cease her accusations against Berne—don't you see? He'd want you to do it."

That finished her resistance. She made him repeat all his directions, precautions for secrecy.

"I wish I could tell you how important it is," he said. "And keep this in mind always: I rely on your paying her the money without even a suspicion of it getting abroad. If accidents happen and you're seen entering the Walman, what more natural than that you want to ask this woman the meaning of her vague threats against—against Sloanehurst?—But of money, your real object, not a word! Nobody's to have a hint of it."

"Oh, yes; I see the necessity of that." But she was distressed. "Suppose she refuses?"

Her altered frame of mind, an eagerness now to succeed with the plan she had at first refused, brought him again his thought of yesterday: "If she were put to it—if she could save only one and had to choose between father and fiancé, her choice would be for the fiancé."

He answered her question. "She won't refuse," he declared, with a confidence she could not doubt. "If I thought she would, I'd almost be willing to say we'd never find the man who killed her daughter."

"When I think of Russell's alibi—"

"Have we mentioned Russell?" he protested, laughing away her fears. "Anyway, his old alibi's no good—if that's what's troubling you. Wait and see!"

He was in high good humour.

In that same hour the woman for whom he had planned this trap was busy with a scheme of her own. Her object was to form an alliance with Sheriff Crown. That gentleman, to use his expressive phrase, had been "putting her over the jumps" for the past forty minutes, bringing to the work of cross-questioning her all the intelligence, craftiness and logic at his command. The net result of his fusillade of interrogatories, however, was exceedingly meagre.

As he sat, caressing his chin and thrusting forward his bristly moustache, Mrs. Brace perceived in his eyes a confession of failure. Although he was far from suspecting it, he presented to her keen scrutiny an amusing figure. She observed that his shoulders drooped, and that, as he slowly produced a handkerchief and mopped his forehead, his movements were eloquent of gloom.

In fact, Mr. Crown felt himself at a loss. He had come to the end of his resourcefulness in the art of probing for facts. He was about to take his departure, with the secret realization that he had learned nothing new—unless an increased admiration of Mrs. Brace's sharpness of wit might be catalogued as knowledge.

She put his thought into language.

"You see, Mr. Crown, you're wasting your time shouting at me, bullying me, accusing me of protecting the murderer of my own daughter."

There was a new note in her voice, a hint, ever so slight, of a willingness to be friendly. He was not insensible to it. Hearing it, he put himself on guard, wondering what it portended.

"I didn't say that," he contradicted, far from graciousness. "I said you knew a whole lot more about the murder than you'd tell—tell me anyway."

"But why should I want to conceal anything that might bring the man to justice?"

"Blessed if I know!" he conceded, not without signs of irritation.

So far as he could see, not a feature of her face changed. The lifted eyebrows were still high upon her forehead, interrogative and mocking; the restless, gleaming eyes still drilled into various parts of his person and attire; the thin lips continued their moving pictures of contempt. And yet, he saw, too, that she presented to him now another countenance.

The change was no more than a shadow; and the shadow was so light that he could not be sure of its meaning. He thought it was friendliness, but that opinion was dulled by recurrence of his admiration of her "smartness." He feared some imposition.

"You've adopted Mr. Hastings' absurd theory," she said, as if she wondered. "You've subscribed to it without question."

"What theory?"

"That I know who the guilty man is."

"Well?" He was still on guard.

"It surprises me—that's all—a man of your intellect, your originality."

She sighed, marvelling at this addition to life's conundrums.

"Why?" he asked, bluntly.

"I should never have thought you'd put yourself in that position before the public. I mean, letting him lead you around by the nose—figuratively."

Mr. Crown started forward in his chair, eyes popped. He was indignant and surprised.

"Is that what they're saying?" he demanded.

"Naturally," she said, and with the one word laid it down as an impossibility that "they" could have said anything else. "That's what the reporters tell me."

"Well, I'll be—dog-goned!" The knuckle-like chin dropped. "They're saying that, are they?"

Disturbed as he was, he noticed that she regarded him with apparently genuine interest—that, perhaps, she added to her interest a regret that he had displayed no originality in the investigation, a man of his intellect!

"They couldn't understand why you were playing Hastings' game," she proceeded, "playing it to his smallest instructions."

"Hastings' game! What the thunder are they talking about? What do they mean, his game?"

"His desire to keep suspicion away from the Sloanes and Mr. Webster. That's what they hired him for—isn't it?"

"I guess it is—by gravy!" Mr. Crown's long-drawn sigh was distinctly tremulous.

"That old man pockets his fee when he throws Gene Russell into jail. Why, then, isn't it his game to convince you of Gene's guilt? Why isn't it his game to persuade you of my secret knowledge of Gene's guilt? Why—"

"So, that's—"

"Let me say what I started," she in turn interrupted him. "As one of the reporters pointed out, why isn't it his game to try to make a fool of you?"

The smile with which she recommended that rumour to his attention incensed him further. It patronized him. It said, as openly as if she had spoken the words: "I'm really very sorry for you."

He dropped his hands to his widespread knees, slid forward to the edge of his chair, thrust his face closer to hers, peered into her hard face for her meaning.

"Making a fool of me, is he?" he said in the brutal key of unrepressed rage.

A quick motion of her lifted brows, a curve of her lower lip—indubitably, a new significance of expression—stopped his outburst.

"By George!" he said, taken aback. "By George!" he repeated, this time in a coarse exultation. He thrust himself still closer to her, certain now of her meaning.

"What do you know?" He lowered his voice and asked again: "Mrs. Brace, what do you know?"

She moved back, farther from him. She was not to be rushed into—anything. She made him appreciate the difficulty of "getting next" to her. He no longer felt fear of her imposing on him—she had just exposed, for his benefit, how Hastings had played on his credulity! He felt grateful to her for that. His only anxiety now was that she might change her mind, might refuse him the assistance which that new and subtle expression had promised a moment ago.

"If I thought you'd use—" she began, broke off, and looked past his shoulder at the opposite wall, the pupils of her eyes sharp points of light, lips drawn to a line almost invisible.

Her evident prudence fired his eagerness.

"If I'd do what?" he asked. "If you thought I'd—what?"

"Let me think," she requested.

He changed his posture, with a great show of watching the sunset sky, and stole little glances at her smooth, untroubled face. He believed now that she could put him on the trail of the murderer. He confessed to himself, unreservedly, that Hastings had tricked him, held him up to ridicule—to the ridicule of a nation, for this crime held the interest of the entire country. But here was his chance for revenge! With this "smart" woman's help, he would outwit Hastings!

"If you'd use my ideas confidentially," she said at last, eying him as if she speculated on his honesty; "if I were sure that—"

"Why can't you be sure of it?" he broke in. "My job is to catch the man who killed your daughter. I've got two jobs. The other is to show up old Hastings! Why wouldn't I do as you ask—exactly as you ask?"

She tantalized him.

"And remember that what I say is ideas only, not knowledge?"

"Sure! Certainly, Mrs. Brace."

"And, even when you arrest the right man, say nothing of what you owe me for my suggestions? You're the kind of man to want to do that sort of thing—give me credit for helping you."

Even that pleased him.

"If you specify silence, I give you my word on it," he said, with a fragment of the pompous manner he had brought into the apartment more than an hour ago.

"You'll take my ideas, my theory, work on it and never bring me into it—in any way? If you make that promise, I'll tell you what I think, what I'm certain is the answer to this puzzle."

"Win or lose, right or wrong idea, you have my oath on it."

"Very well!" She said that with the air of one embarking on a tremendous venture and scorning all its possibilities of harm. "I shall trust you fully.—First, let me sketch all the known facts, everything connected with the tragedy, and everything I know concerning the conduct of the affected individuals since."

He was leaning far toward her once more, a child-like impatience stamped on his face. As she proceeded, his admiration grew.

For this, there was ample ground. The newspaper paragraph Hastings had read that morning commenting on her mastery of all the details of the crime had scarcely done her justice. Before she concluded, Crown had heard from her lips little incidents that had gone over his head. She put new and accurate meaning into facts time and time again, speaking with the particularity and vividness of an eye-witness.

"Now," she said, having reconstructed the crime and described the subsequent behaviour of the tragedy's principal actors; "now who's guilty?"

"Exactly," echoed Crown, with a click in his throat. "Who's guilty? What's your theory?"

She was silent, eyes downcast, her hands smoothing the black, much-worn skirt over her lean knees. Recital of the gruesome story, the death of her only child, had left her unmoved, had not quickened her breathing.

"In telling you that," she resumed, her restless eyes striking his at rapid intervals, "I think I'll put you in a position to get the right man—if you'll act."

"Oh, I'll act!" he declared, largely. "Don't bother your head about that!"

"Of course, it's only a theory—"

"Yes; I know! And I'll keep it to myself."

"Very well. Arthur Sloane is prostrated, can't be interviewed. He can't be interviewed, for the simple reason that he's afraid he'll tell what he knows. Why is he afraid of that? Because he knows too much, for his own comfort, and too much for his daughter's comfort. How does he know it? Because he saw enough night before last to leave him sure of the murderer's identity.

"He was the man who turned on the light, showing Webster and Judge Wilton bending over Mildred's body. It occurred at a time when usually he is in his first sound sleep—from bromides. Something must have happened to awake him, an outcry, something. And yet, he says he didn't see them—Wilton and Webster."

"By gravy!" exclaimed the sheriff, awe-struck.

"Either," she continued, "Arthur Sloane saw the murder done, or he looked out in time to see who the murderer was. The facts substantiate that. They are corroborated by his subsequent behaviour. Immediately after the murder he was in a condition that couldn't be explained by the mere fact that he's a sufferer from chronic nervousness. When Hastings asked him to take a handkerchief, he would have fallen to the ground but for the judge's help. He couldn't hold an electric torch. And, ever since, he's been in bed, afraid to talk. Why, he even refused to talk to Hastings, the man he's retained for the family's protection!"

"He did, did he! How do you know that, Mrs. Brace?"

"Isn't it enough that I know it—or advance it as a theory?"

"Did—I thought, possibly, Jarvis, the valet, told you."

She ignored that.

"Now, as to the daughter of the house. There was only one possible reason for Lucille Sloane's hiring Hastings: she was afraid somebody in the house, Webster, of course, would be arrested. Being in love with him, she never would have suspected him unless there had been concrete, undeniable evidence of his guilt. Do you grasp that reasoning?"

"Sure, I do!" Mr. Crown condemned himself. "What I'm wondering is why I didn't see it long ago."

"She, too, you recall, was looking out of a window—on that side of the house—scarcely fifteen yards from where the crime was done. It's not hard to believe that she saw what her father saw: the murder or the murderer.

"Mr. Crown, if you can make her or her father talk, you'll get the truth of this thing, the truth and the murderer.

"And look at Judge Wilton's part. You asked me why I went to his office this morning. I went because I'm sure he knows the truth. Didn't he stay right at Webster's side when old Hastings interviewed Webster yesterday? Why? To keep Webster from letting out, in his panic, a secret which both of them knew."

The sheriff's admiration by this time was boundless. He felt driven to give it expression.

"Mrs. Brace, you're a loo-loo! A loo-loo, by gravy! Sure, that was his reason. He couldn't have had any other!"

"As for Webster himself," she carried on her exposition, without emotion, without the slightest recognition of her pupil's praise, "he proves the correctness of everything we've said, so far. That secret which the judge feared he would reveal, that secret which old Hastings was blundering after—that secret, Mr. Crown, was such a danger to him that, to escape the questioning of even stupid old Hastings, he could do nothing but crumple up on the floor and feign illness, prostration. Why, don't you see, he was afraid to talk!"

"Everything you say hits the mark!" agreed Crown, smiling happily. "Centre-shots! Centre-shots! You've been right from the very beginning. You tried to tell me all this yesterday morning, and, fool that I was—fool that Hastings was!" He switched to a summary of what she had put into his mind: "It's right! Webster killed her, and Sloane and his daughter saw him at it. Even Wilton knows it—and he a judge! It seems impossible. By gravy! he ought to be impeached."

A new idea struck him. Mrs. Brace, imperturbable, exhibiting no elation, was watching him closely. She saw his sudden change of countenance. He had thought: "She didn't reason this out. Russell saw the murder—the coward—and he's told her. He ran away from—"

Another suspicion attacked him: "But that was Jarvis' night off. Has she seen Jarvis?"

Impelled to put this fresh bewilderment into words, he was stayed by the restless, brilliant eyes with which she seemed to penetrate his lumbering mind. He was afraid of losing her cooperation. She was too valuable an ally to affront. He kept quiet.

She brought him back to her purpose.

"Then, you agree with me? You think Webster's guilty?"

"Think!" He almost shouted his contempt of the inadequate word. "Think! I know! Guilty? The man's black with guilt."

"I'm sure of it," she said, curiously skilful in surrendering to him all credit for that vital discovery. "What are you going to do—now that you know?"

"Make him talk, turn him inside out! Playing sick, is he! I'm going back to Sloanehurst this evening. I'm going to start something. You can take this from me: Webster'll loosen that tongue of his before another sun rises!"

But that was not her design.

"You can't do it," she objected, her voice heavy with disappointment. "Dr. Garnet, your own coroner, says questioning will kill him. Dr. Garnet's as thoroughly fooled as Hastings, and," she prodded him with suddenly sharp tone, "you."

"That's right." He was crestfallen, plucking at his chin. "That's hard to get around. But I've got to get around it! I've got to show results, Mrs. Brace. People, some of the papers even, are already hinting that I'm too easy on a rich man and his friend."

"Yes," she said, evenly. "And you told—I understood you'd act, on our theory."

"I've got to! I've got to act!"

His confusion was manifest. He did not know what to do, and he was silent, hoping for a suggestion from her. She let him wait. The pause added to his embarrassment.

"What would—that is," he forced himself to the appeal, "I was wondering—anything occur to you? See any way out of it?"

"Of course, I know nothing about such procedure," she replied to that, slowly, as if she groped for a new idea. "But, if you got the proof from somewhere else, enough to warrant the arrest of Webster—" Her smile deprecated her probable ineptness. "If Arthur Sloane—"

He fairly fell upon the idea.

"Right!" he said, clapping his hands together. "Sloane's no dying man, is he? And he knows the whole story. Right you are, Mrs. Brace! He can shake and tremble and whine all he pleases, but tonight he's my meat—my meat, right! Talk? You bet he'll talk!"

She considered, looking at the opposite wall. He was convinced that she examined the project, viewing it from the standpoint of his interest, seeking possible dangers of failure. Nevertheless, he hurried her decision.

"It's the thing to do, isn't it?"

"I should think so," she said at last. "You, with your mental forceful-ness, your ability as a questioner—why, I don't see how you can fail to get at what he knows. Beside, you have the element of surprise on your side. That will go far toward sweeping him off his feet."

He was again conscious of his debt of gratitude to this woman, and tried to voice it.

"This is the first time," he declared, big with confidence, "I've felt that I had the right end of this case."

When she had closed the door on him, she went back to the living room and set back in its customary place the chair he had occupied. Her own was where it always belonged. From there she went into the bathroom and, as Hastings had seen her do before, drew a glass of water which she drank slowly.

Then, examining her hard, smooth face in the bedroom mirror, she said aloud:

"Pretty soon, now, somebody will talk business—with me."

There was no elation in her voice. But her lips were, for a moment, thick and wet, changing her countenance into a picture of inordinate greed.

XV

In Arthur Sloane's Room

Hastings went back to Sloanehurst that evening for another and more forceful attempt to argue Arthur Sloane into frankness. Like Mrs. Brace, he could not get away from the definite conclusion that Lucille's father was silent from fear of telling what he knew. Moreover, he realized that, without a closer connection with Sloane, his own handling of the case was seriously impeded.

Lucille was on the front porch, evidently waiting for him, although he had not notified her in advance of his visit. She went hurriedly down the steps and met him on the walk. When he began an apology for having to annoy her so frequently, she cut short his excuses.

"Oh, but I'm glad you're here—so glad! We need your help. The sheriff's here."

She put her hand on his coat sleeve; he could feel the tremour of it as she pulled, unconsciously, on the cloth. She turned toward the verandah steps.

"What's he doing?" he asked, detaining her.

"He's in father's room," she said in feverish haste, "asking him all sorts of questions, saying ridiculous things. Really, I'm afraid—for father's health! Can't you go in now?"

"Couldn't Judge Wilton manage him? Isn't the judge here?"

"No. He came over at dinner time; but he went back to the Randalls'. Father didn't feel up to talking to him."

Crown, she explained, had literally forced his way into the bedroom, disregarding her protests and paying no attention to the pretence of physical resistance displayed by Jarvis.

"The man seems insane!" she said. "I want you to make him leave father's room—please!"

She halted near the library door, leaving the matter in Hastings' hands. Since entering the house he had heard Crown's voice, raised to the key of altercation; and now, when he stepped into Sloane's room, the rush of words continued.

The sheriff, unaware of the newcomer, stood near the bed, emphasizing his speech with restless arms and violent motions of his head, as if to galvanize into response the still and prostrate form before him. On the opposite side of the bed stood the sepulchral Jarvis, flashing malign looks at Crown, but chiefly busy, with unshaking hands, preparing a beverage of some sort for the sick man.

Sloane lay on his back, eyes closed, face under the full glare of the reading light. His expression indicated both boredom and physical suffering.

"—have to make an arrest!" Crown was saying. "You're making me take that action—ain't you? I come in here, considerate as I know how to be, and I ask you for a few facts. Do you give 'em to me? Not by a long shot! You lie there in that bed, and talk about leaping angels, and say I bore you! Well, Mr. Sloane, that won't get you a thing! You're where I said you were: it's either Webster that will be arrested—or yourself! Now, I'm giving you another chance. I'm asking you what you saw; and you can tell me—or take the consequences!"

Hastings thought: "He's up that gum stump of his again, and don't know how to quit talking."

Sloane made no answer.

"Well," thundered Crown. "I'm asking you!"

"Moaning martyrs!" Sloane protested in a thin, querulous tone. "Jarvis, the bromide."

"All right!" the sheriff delivered his ultimatum. "I'll stick to what I said. Webster may be too sick to talk, but not too sick to have a warrant served on him. He'll be arrested because you won't tell me—"

Hastings spoke then.

"Gentlemen!" he greeted pleasantly. "Mr. Sloane, good evening. Mr. Sheriff—am I interrupting a private conference?"

"Fiery fiends!" wailed Sloane. "Another!"

Hastings gave his attention to Crown. He was certain that the man, balked by Sloane's refusal to "talk," would welcome an excuse for leaving the room.

"Let me see you a moment, will you?" He put a hand on the sheriff's shoulder, persuading: "It's important, right now."

"But I want to know what Mr. Sloane's going to say," Crown blustered. "If he'll tell—"

Hastings stopped him with a whisper: "That's exactly what he'll do—soon!"

He led the sheriff into the hall. They went into the parlour.

"Now," Hastings began, in genial tone; "did you get anything from him?"

"Not a dad-blamed thing!" Crown was still blustery. "But he'll talk before I'm through! You can put your little bets down on that!"

"All right. You've had your chance at him. Better let me see him."

Crown looked his distrust. He was thinking of Mrs. Brace's warning that this man had made a fool of him.

"I'm not trying to put anything over on you," the detective assured him. "Fact is, I'm out here for the newspaper men. They've had nothing from him; they've asked me to get his story. I'll give it to you before I see them. What do you say?"

Crown still hesitated.

"If, after you've heard it," Hastings added, "you want to question him further, you can do it, of course. But this way we take two shots at it."

To that, the other finally agreed.

Hastings found Sloane smoking a cigarette, his eyes still closed. Jarvis was behind a screen near the door, now and then clinking glass against glass as he worked.

The old man took a chair near the bed and waited for Sloane to speak. He waited a long time. Finally, the invalid looked at him from under lowered lids, slyly, like a child peeping. Hastings returned the look with a pleasant smile, his shrewd eyes sparkling over the rims of his spectacles.

"Well!" Sloane said at last, in a whiney tone. "What do you want?"

"First," Hastings apologized, "I want to say how sorry I am I didn't make myself clearly understood night before last when I told Miss Sloane I'd act as mouthpiece for this household. I didn't mean I could invent a statement for each of you, or for any of you. What I did mean amounts to this: if you, for instance, would tell me what you know—all you know—about this murder, I could relay it to the reporters—and to the sheriff, who's been annoying you so this evening. As—"

"Flat-headed fiends!" Sloane cut in, writhing under the light coverlet. "Another harangue!"

Hastings kept his temper.

"No harangue about it. But it's to come to this, Mr. Sloane: you're handicapping me, and the reporters and the sheriff don't trust you."

"Why? Why don't they trust me?" shrilled Sloane, writhing again.

"Ill tell you in a very few words: because you refused to testify at the inquest yesterday, giving illness as an excuse. That's one reason. The—"

"Howling helions! Wasn't I ill? Didn't I have enough to make me ill?—Jarvis, a little whiskey!"

"Dr. Garnet hasn't told them so—the reporters. He won't tell them so. In fact," Hastings said, with less show of cordiality, "from all he said to me, I gather he doesn't think you an ill man—that is, dangerously ill."

"And because of that, they say what, these reporters, this sheriff? What?"

"They're in ugly mood, Mr. Sloane. They're saying you're trying to protect—somebody—by keeping still about a thing which you should be the first to haul into daylight. That's it—in a nutshell."

Sloane had stopped trembling. He sat up in the bed and stared at the detective out of steady, hard eyes. He waved away the whiskey Jarvis held toward him.

"And you want what, Mr. Hastings?" he inquired, a curiously effective sarcasm in his voice.

"A statement covering every second from the time you woke up Saturday night until you saw the body."

"A statement!—Reporters!" He was snarling on that. "What's got into you, anyway? What are you trying to do—make people suspect me of the murder-make 'em suspect Berne?"

He threw away the cigarette and shook his fist at Hastings. He gulped twice before he could speak again; he seemed on the point of choking.

"In an ugly mood, are they? Well, they can stay in an ugly mood. You, too! And that hydrophobiac sheriff! Quivering and crucified saints! I've had enough of all of you—all of you, understand! Get out of here! Get out!"

Although his voice was shrill, there was no sound of weakness in it. The trembling that attacked him was the result of anger, not of nervousness.

Hastings rose, astounded by the outbreak.

"I'm afraid you don't realize the seriousness of—"

"Oh, get out of here!" Sloane interrupted again. "You've imposed on my daughter with your talk of being helpful, and all that rot, but you can't hoodwink me. What the devil do you mean by letting that sheriff come in here and subject me to all this annoyance and shock? You'd save us from unpleasantness!"

He spoke more slowly now, as if he cudgelled his brain for the most biting sarcasm, the most unbearable insolence.

"Don't realize the seriousness!—Flat-headed fiends!—Are you any nearer the truth now than you were at the start?—Try to understand this, Mr. Hastings: you're discharged, fired! From now on, I'm in charge of what goes on in this house. If there's any trouble to be avoided, I'll attend to it. Get that!—and get out!"

Hastings, opening his mouth for angry retort, checked himself. He stood a moment silent, shaken by the effort it cost him to maintain his self-control.

"Humph!" Sloane's nasal, twangy exclamation was clearly intended to provoke him further.

But, without a word, he turned and left the room. Passing the screen near the door, he heard Jarvis snicker, a discreet echo of Sloane's goading ridicule.

On his way back to the parlour, the old man made up his mind to discount Sloane's behaviour.

"I've got to take a chance," he counselled himself, "but I know I'm right in doing it. A big responsibility—but I'm right!"

Then he submitted this report:

"He says nothing new, Crown. Far as I can make out, nothing unusual waked him up that night—except chronic nervousness; he turned on that light to find some medicine; he knew nothing of the murder until Judge Wilton called him."

"Humph!" growled Crown. "And you fall for that!"

Hastings eyed him sternly. "It's the statement I'm going to give to the reporters."

The sheriff was silent, irresolute. Hastings congratulated himself on his earlier deduction: that Crown, unable to frighten Sloane into communicativeness, was thankful for an excuse to withdraw.

Hendricks had reported the two-hour conference between Crown and Mrs. Brace late that afternoon. Hastings decided now: "The man's in cahoots with her. His ally! And he won't act until he's had another session with her.—And she won't advise an arrest for a day or two anyway. Her game is to make him play on Sloane's nerves for a while. She advises threats, not arrests—which suits me, to a T!"

He fought down a chuckle, thinking of that alliance.

Crown corroborated his reasoning.

"All right, Hastings," he said doggedly. "I'm not going back to his room. I gave him his chance. He can take the consequences."

"What consequences?"

"I'd hardly describe 'em to his personal representative, would I? But you can take this from me: they'll come soon enough—and rough enough!"

Hastings made no reference to having been dismissed by Sloane. He was glad when Crown changed the subject.

"Hastings, you saw the reporters this afternoon—I've been wondering—they asked me—did they ask you whether you suspected the valet—Jarvis?"

"Of what?"

"Killing her."

"No; they didn't ask me."

"Funny," said Crown, ill at ease. "They asked me."

"So you said," Hastings reminded, looking hard at him.

"Well!" Crown blurted it out. "Do you suspect him? Are you working on that line—at all?"

Hastings paused. He had no desire to mislead him. And yet, there was no reason for confiding in him—and delay was at present the Hastings plan.

"I'll tell you, Crown," he said, finally; "I'll work on any line that can lead to the guilty man.—What do you know?"

"Who? Me?" Crown's tone indicated the absurdity of suspecting Jarvis. "Not a thing."

But it gave Hastings food for thought. Was Mrs. Brace in communication with Jarvis? And did Crown know that? Was it possible that Crown wanted to find out whether Hastings was having Jarvis shadowed? How much of a fool was the woman making of the sheriff, anyway?

Another thing puzzled him: why did Mrs. Brace suspect Arthur Sloane of withholding the true story of what he had seen the night of the murder? Hastings' suspicion, amounting to certainty, came from his knowledge that the man's own daughter thought him deeply involved in the crime. But Mrs. Brace—was she clever enough to make that deduction from the known facts? Or did she have more direct information from Sloanehurst than he had thought possible?

He decided not to leave the sheriff entirely subject to her schemes and suggestions. He would give Mr. Crown something along another line—a brake, as it were, on impulsive action.

"You talk about arresting Webster right away—or Sloane," he began, suddenly confiding. "You wouldn't want to make a mistake—would you?"

Crown rose to that. "Why? What do you know—specially?"

"Well, not so much, maybe. But it's worth thinking about. I'll give you the facts—confidentially, of course.—Hub Hill's about a hundred yards from this house, on the road to Washington. When automobiles sink into it hub-deep, they come out with a lot of mud on their wheels—black, loamy mud. Ain't any other mud like that Hub Hill mud anywhere near here. It's just special and peculiar to Hub Hill. That so?"

"Yes," agreed Crown, absorbed.

"All right. How, then, did Eugene Russell keep black, Hub Hill mud on his shoes that night if he went the four miles on foot to where Otis picked him up?"

"Eh?" said Crown, chin fallen.

"By the time he'd run four miles, his shoes would have been covered with the red mud of that mile of 'dirt road' or the thin, grey mud of the three miles of pike—wouldn't they? They'd have thrown off that Hub Hill mud pretty quick, wouldn't they?"

"Thunder!" marvelled Crown. "That's right! And those shoes were in his room; I saw 'em." He gurgled, far back in his throat. "Say! How did he get from Hub Hill to where Otis picked him up?"

"That's what I say," declared Hastings, very bland. "How?"

To Lucille, after Crown's departure, the detective declared his intention to "stand by" her, to stay on the case. He repeated his statement of yesterday: he suspected too much, and knew too little, to give it up.

He told her of the responsibility he had assumed in giving the sheriff the fictitious Sloane statement. "That is, it's not fictitious, in itself; it's what your father has been saying. But I told Crown, and I'm going to tell the newspaper men, that he says it's all he knows, really. And I hate to do it—because, honestly, Miss Sloane, I don't think it is all. I'm afraid he's deceiving us."

She did not contradict that; it was her own opinion.

"However," the old man made excuse, "I had to do it—in view of things as they are. And he's got to stick to it, now that I've made it 'official,' so to speak. Do you think he will?"

She did not see why not. She would explain to him the importance, the necessity, of that course.

"He's so mistaken in what he's doing!" she said. "I don't understand him—really. You know how devoted to me he is. He called me into his room again an hour or two ago and tried to comfort me. He said he had reason to know everything would come out as it should. But he looked so—so uncertain!—Oh, Mr. Hastings, who did kill that woman?"

"I think I'll be able to prove who did it—let's see," he spoke with a light cheerfulness, and at the same time with sincerity; "I'll be able to prove it in less than a week after Mrs. Brace takes that money from you."

She said nothing to that, and he leaned forward sharply, peering at her face, illegible to him in the darkness of the verandah.

"So much depends on that, on you," he added. "You won't fail me—tomorrow?"

"I'll do my best," she said, earnestly, struggling against depression.

"She must take that money," he declared with great emphasis. "She must!"

"And you think she will?"

"Miss Sloane, I know she will," he said, a fatherly encouragement in his voice. "I'm seldom mistaken in people; and I know I've judged this woman correctly. Money's her weakness. Love of it has destroyed her already. Offering this bribe to anybody else situated as she is would be ridiculous—but she—she'll take it."

Lucille sat a long time on the verandah after Hastings had gone. She was far more depressed than he had suspected; she had to endure so much, she thought—the suspense, which grew heavier as time went by; the notoriety; Berne Webster still in danger of his life; her father's inexplicable pose of indifference toward everything; the suspicions of the newspapers and the public of both her father and Berne; and the waiting, waiting, waiting—for what?

A little moan escaped her.

What if Mrs. Brace did take the marked money? What would that show? That she was acting with criminal intent, Hastings had said. But he had another and more definite object in urging her to this undertaking; he expected from it a vital development which he had not explained—she was sure. She worried with that idea.

Her confidence in Hastings had been without qualification. But what was he doing? Anything? Judge Wilton was forever saying, "Trust Hastings; he's the man for this case." And that was his reputation; people declared that, if anybody could get to the bottom of all this mystery, he could. Yet, two whole days had passed since the murder, and he had just said another week might be required to work out his plan of detection—whatever that plan was.

Another week of this! She put her hot palms to her hotter temples, striving for clarity of thought. But she was dazed by her terror—her isolated terror, for some of her thoughts were such that she could share them with nobody—not even Hastings.

"If the sheriff makes no arrest within the next few days, I'll be out of the woods," he had told her. "Delay is what I want."

There, again, was discouragement, for here was the sheriff threatening to serve a warrant on Berne within the next twenty-four hours! She had heard Crown make the threat, and to her it had seemed absolutely final: unless her father revealed something which Crown wanted, whether her father knew it or not, Berne was to be subjected to this humiliation, this added blow to his chance for recovery!

She sprang up, throwing her hands wide and staring blindly at the stars.

The woman whom she was to bribe cast a deep shadow on her imagination. Sharing the feeling of many others, she had reached the reluctant conclusion that Mrs. Brace in some way knew more than anybody else about the murder and its motives. It was, she told herself, a horrid feeling, and without reason. But she could not shake it off. To her, Mrs. Brace was a figure of sinister power, an agent of ugliness, waiting to do evil—waiting for what?

By a great effort, she steadied her jangled nerves. Hastings was counting on her. And work—even work in the dark—was preferable to this idleness, this everlasting summing-up of frightful possibilities without a ray of hope. She would do her best to make that woman take the money!

Tomorrow she would be of real service to Berne Webster—she would atone, in some small measure, for the sorrow she had brought upon him, discarding him because of empty gossip!—Would he continue to love her?—Perhaps, if she had not discarded him, Mildred Brace would not have been murdered.

A groan escaped her. She fled into the house, away from her thoughts.

XVI

The Bribe

It was nine o'clock the following evening when Lucille Sloane, sure that she had entered the Walman unobserved, rang the bell of Mrs. Brace's apartment. Her body felt remarkably light and facile, as if she moved in a tenuous, half-real atmosphere. There were moments when she had the sensation of floating. Her brain worked with extraordinary rapidity. She was conscious of an unusually resourceful intelligence, and performed a series of mental gymnastics, framing in advance the sentences she would use in the interview confronting her.

The constant thought at the back of her brain was that she would succeed; she would speak and act in such a way that Mrs. Brace would take the money. She was buoyed by a fierce determination to be repaid for all the suspense, all the agony of heart, that had weighed her down throughout this long, leaden-footed day—the past twenty-four hours unproductive of a single enlightening incident.

Mrs. Brace opened the door and, with a scarcely perceptible nod of the head, motioned her into the living room. Neither of them spoke until they had seated themselves on the chairs by the window. Even then, the silence was prolonged, until Lucille realized that her tongue was dry and uncomfortably large for her mouth. An access of trembling shook her. She tried to smile and knew that her lips were twisting in a ghastly grin.

Mrs. Brace moved slowly to and fro on the armless rocker, her swift, appraising eyes taking in her visitor's distress. The smooth face wore its customary, inexpressive calm. Lucille, striving desperately to arrive at some opinion of what the woman thought, saw that she might as well try to find emotion in a statue.

"I—I," the girl finally attained a quick, flurried utterance, "want to thank you for—for having this—this talk with me."

"What do you want to talk about, Miss Sloane?"

The low, metallic voice was neither friendly nor hostile. It expressed, more than anything else, a sardonic, bullying self-sufficiency.

It both angered and encouraged Lucille. She perceived the futility of polite, introductory phrases here; she could go straight to her purpose, be brutally frank. She gave Mrs. Brace a brilliant, disarming smile, a proclamation of fellowship. Her confidence was restored.

"I'm sure we can talk sensibly together, Mrs. Brace," she explained, dissembling her indignation. "We can get down to business, at once."

"What business?" inquired the older woman, with some of the manner Hastings had seen, an air of lying in wait.

"I said, on the phone, it was something of advantage to you—didn't I?"

"Yes; you said that."

"And, of course, I want something from you."

"Naturally."

"I'll tell you what it is." Lucille spoke now with cool precision, as yet untouched by the horror she had expected to feel. "It's a matter of money."

Mrs. Brace's tongue came out to the edge of the thin line of her lips. Her nostrils quivered, once, to the sharply indrawn breath. Her eyes were more furtive.

"Money?" she echoed. "For what?"

"There's no good of my making long explanations, Mrs. Brace," Lucille said. "I've read the newspapers, every line of them, about—our trouble. And I saw the references to your finances, your lack of money."

"Yes?" Mrs. Brace's right hand lay on her lap; the thumb of it began to move against the forefinger rapidly, the motion a woman makes in feeling the texture of cloth—or the trick of a bank clerk separating paper money.

"Yes. I read, also, what you said about the tragedy. Today I noticed that the only note of newness in the articles in the papers came from you—from your saying that 'in a few days, three or four at the outside'—that was your language, I'm quite sure—you'd produce evidence on which an arrest would be made. I've intelligence enough to see that the public's interest in you is so great, the sympathy for you is so great, that your threats—I mean, predictions, or opinions—colour everything that's written by the reporters. You see?"

"Do I see what?"

Despite her excellent pose of waiting with nothing more than a polite interest, Lucille saw in her a pronounced alteration. That was not so much in her face as in her body. Her limbs had a look of rigidity.

"Don't you see what I mean?" Lucille insisted. "I see that you can make endless trouble for us—for all of us at Sloanehurst. You can make people believe Mr. Webster guilty, and that father and I are shielding him. People listen to what you say. They seem to be on your side."

"Well?"

"I wondered if you wouldn't stop your interviews—your accusations?"

The younger woman's eagerness, evident now in the variety of her gestures and the rapid procession of pallour and flush across her cheeks, persuaded Mrs. Brace that Lucille was acting on an impulse of her own, not as an agent to carry out another's well designed scheme. The older woman, at that idea, felt safe. She asked:

"And you want—what?"

"I've come here to ask you to tell me all you know, or to be quiet altogether."

"I'm afraid I don't understand—fully," returned Mrs. Brace, with an exaggerated bewilderment. "Tell all I know?"

"That is, if you do know anything you haven't told!" Lucille urged her. "Oh, don't you see? I'm saying to you that I want to put an end to this dreadful suspense!"

Mrs. Brace laughed disagreeably; her face was harder, less human. "You mean I'm amusing myself, exerting myself needlessly, as a matter of spite? Do you mean to tell me that?"

"No! No!" Lucille denied, impatient with herself for lack of clearness. "I mean I'm sure you're attacking an innocent man. And I'm willing, I'm anxious—oh, I hope so much, Mrs. Brace—to make an agreement with you—a financial arrangement—" She paused the fractional part of a second on that; and, seeing that the other did not resent the term, she added: "to pay you to stop it. Isn't that clear?"

"Yes; that's clear."

"Understand me, please. What I ask is that you say nothing more to the reporters, the sheriff or the Washington police, that will have the effect of hounding them on against Mr. Webster. I want to eliminate from the situation all the influence you've exerted to make Mr. Crown believe Mr. Webster's guilty and my father's protecting him."

"Let me think," Mrs. Brace said, coolly.

Lucille exulted inwardly, "She'll do it! She'll do it!" The hard eyes dissected her eager face. The girl drew back in her chair, thinking now: "She suspects who sent me!"

At last, the older woman spoke:

"The detective, Hastings, would never have allowed you to come here, Miss Sloane.—Excuse my frankness," she interjected, with a smile she meant to be friendly; "but you're frank with me; we're not mincing matters; and I have to be careful.—He'd have warned you that your errand's practical confession of your knowledge of something incriminating Berne Webster. If you didn't suspect the man even more strongly than I do, you'd never have been driven to—this."

She leaned the rocker back and crossed her knees, the movement throwing into high relief the hard lankness of her figure. She gazed at the wall, over Lucille's head, as she dealt with the possibilities that presented themselves to her analysis. Her manner was that of a certain gloating enjoyment, a thinly covered, semi-orderly greediness.

"She's not even thinking of her daughter," Lucille thought, and went pale a moment. "She's as bad as Mr. Hastings said—worse!"

"Then, too," Mrs. Brace continued, "your father discharged him last night."

Lucille remembered the detective's misgivings about Jarvis; how else had this woman found that out?

"And you've taken matters into your own hands.—Did your father send you here—to me?"

"Why, no!"

The other smiled slyly, the tip of her tongue again visible, her eyebrows high in interrogation. "Of course," she said; "you wouldn't tell me if he had. He would have warned you against that admission."

"It's Mr. Webster about whom I am most concerned," Lucille reminded, sharpness in her vibrant young voice. "My father's being annoyed is merely incidental."

"Oh, of course! Of course," Mrs. Brace grinned, with broad sarcasm.

Lucille started. The meaning of that could not be misunderstood; she charged that the money was offered at Arthur Sloane's instigation and that the concern for Berne Webster was merely pretence.

Mrs. Brace saw her anger, and placated it:

"Don't mind me, Miss Sloane. A woman who's had to endure what I have—well, she doesn't always think clearly."

"Perhaps not," Lucille assented; but she was aware of a sudden longing to be done with the degrading work. "Now that we understand each other, Mrs. Brace, what do you say?"

Mrs. Brace thought again.

"How much?" she asked at last, her lips thickening. "How much, Miss Sloane, do you think my silence is worth?"

Lucille took a roll of bills from her handbag. The woman's chair slid forward, answering to the forward—leaning weight of her new posture. She was lightly rubbing her palms together, as, with head a little bowed, she stared at the money in the younger woman's hand.

"I have here five hundred dollars," Lucille began.

"What!"

Mrs. Brace said that roughly; and, in violent anger, drew back, the legs of her chair grating on the floor.

For a moment Lucille gazed at her, uncomprehending.

"Oh!" she said, uncertainly. "You mean—it isn't enough?"

"Enough!" Mrs. Brace's rage and disappointment grew, her lowered brows a straight line close down to her eyes.

"But I could get more!" Lucille exclaimed, struggling with disgust. "This," she added, with ready invention, "can serve as a part payment, a promise of—"

"Ah-h!" the older woman exclaimed. "That's different. I misunderstood."

She put down the signals of her wrath, succeeding in that readjustment so promptly that Lucille stared at her in undisguised amazement.

"You must pardon me, Miss Sloane. I thought you were making me the victim of your ridicule, some heartless joke."

"Then, we can come to an agreement? That is, if this money is the first—"

She broke the sentence. Mrs. Brace had put up her hand, and now held her head to one side, listening.

There was a step clearly audible outside, in the main hall. The next moment the doorbell rang. They sat motionless. When the bell rang again, Mrs. Brace informed her with a look that she would not answer it.

But the ringing continued, became a prolonged jangle. It got on Lucille's already strained nerves.

"Suppose you slip into the bedroom," Mrs. Brace whispered.

"Oh, no!" Lucille whispered back.

She was weighed down by black premonition; she hoped Mrs. Brace would not open the door.

The bell rang again.

"You'll have to!" Mrs. Brace said at last. "I won't let anybody in. I have to answer it!"

"You'll send them away—whoever it is—at once?"

"At once. I don't want you seen here, any more than you want to be seen!"

Lucille started toward the bedroom. At the first step she took, Mrs. Brace put a hand on her arm.

"That money!" she demanded, in a low whisper. "I'll take it."

"And do what I asked—stop attacking us?"

"Yes. Yes!"

Lucille gave her the money.

There were no lights in the bedroom. Lucille, for fear of stumbling or making a noise, stood to one side of the door-frame, close to the wall.

Mrs. Brace's footsteps stopped. There was the click of the opening door. Then, there came to Lucille the high-pitched, querulous voice which she had been afraid she would hear.

It was her father's.

XVII

"The Whole Truth"

"Mrs. Brace, good evening.—May I come in?"

Then followed the sound of footsteps, and the closing of the door.

"I shan't detain you long, Mrs. Brace." They were still in the hall. "May I come in?"

"Certainly." The tardy assent was the perfection of indifference.

They entered the living room. Lucille, without using her eyes, knew that her father was standing just within the doorway, glancing around with his slight squint, working his lips nervously, his head thrust forward.

"Ah-h!" his shrill drawl, although he kept it low, carried back to Lucille. "All alone—may I ask?" He went toward the chairs by the window. "That is, I hope to have—well—rather a confidential little talk with you."

Mrs. Brace resumed her place on the armless rocker after she had moved a chair forward for him. Lucille heard it grate on the floor. Certain that he had taken it, she looked into the room. Her intuition was correct; Mrs. Brace had placed it so that his back was turned to both the bedroom door and the door into the entry. This made her escape possible.

The relief she got from the thought was of a violent nature. It came to her like a blow, almost forcing a gasp from her constricted throat. If she could tiptoe without sound a distance of eighteen feet, a matter of six or seven steps, she could leave the apartment without his knowledge.

To that she was doubly urged. In the first place, Hastings' warning drummed upon her brain; he had specified the importance of keeping even her father in ignorance of her errand.

Upon that came another reason for flight, her fear of hearing what her father would say. A wave of nausea weakened her. She bowed down, there in the dark, under the burden of her suspicion: he had come to do, for quite a different reason, what she had done! She kept away from definite analysis of his motive. Fear for Berne, or fear for himself, it was equally horrible to her consideration.

"I admire your spirit, Mrs. Brace," he was saying, in ingratiating tone; "and your shrewdness. I've followed all you said, in the papers. And I'm in hopes that we may—"

He stopped, and Lucille, judging from the thin edges of sounds that she caught, had a mental picture of his peering over his shoulder. He resumed:

"I must apologize, I'm sure. But you'll realize my concern for secrecy—after I've explained. May I—ah-h-h—do you mind if I look about, for possible hearers?"

"It's unnecessary," came the calm, metallic assurance. "I've no objection to your searching my apartment, if you insist." She laughed, a mirthless deprecation of his timidity, and coolly put herself at his disposal in another sentence: "I've sense enough to form an idea of what you'll propose; and I'd scarcely want others to hear it—would I?"

"Ah-h-h!" he drawled, expressing a grudging disposition to accept her assurance. "Certainly not.—Well, that's very reasonable—and obliging, I'm sure."

Again by the thin fringes of sound, Lucille got information of his settling into his chair.

"Why," he began; "why, in the name of all the unfathomable, inscrutable angels—"

"First, Mr. Sloane," Mrs. Brace interrupted him—and Lucille heard the rattle of a newspaper; "as a preface to our—shall we say conference?—our conference, then, let me read you this summary of my position.—That is, if you care to understand my position thoroughly."

She was far from her habitual quietness, rattling the newspaper incessantly. The noise, Lucille realized, would hang as a curtain between her father's ears and the possible sounds of her progress from the bedroom door to the entry.

Stealing a glance into the living room, she saw his back and, over his stooped shoulders, Mrs. Brace's calm face. In that instant, the newspaper shook more violently—enough, she thought, to signal cooperation.

She sickened again at sight of that woman about to dispense bought favours to her father. The impulse to step forth and proclaim her presence rose strongly within her; but she was turned from it by fear that her interruption might produce disastrous results. After all, she was not certain of his intention.

She knew, however, that at any moment he might insist on satisfying himself, by a tour of inspection, that he was safe from being overheard. She hesitated no longer. She would try to get away.

"Look at this, Mr. Sloane, if you please," Mrs. Brace was saying; "notice how the items are made to stand out, each in a paragraph of large type."

She held the paper so that Sloane bent forward, and, against his will, was held to joint perusal while she read aloud. The curtain of protecting noise thus was thickened.

"'That Mrs. Brace has knowledge of the following facts,'" the harsh, colourless voice was reading.

Lucille began her escape. She moved with an agony of precaution, taking steps only a few inches long, her arms held out from her sides to avoid unnecessary rustling of her clothing. She went on the balls of her feet, keeping the heels of her shoes always free of the floor, each step a slow torture.

Her breathing stopped—a hysterical contraction of her chest prevented breathing. Her face burned like fire. Her head felt crowded, as if the blood tried to ooze through the confining scalp. There was a great roaring in her ears. The pulse in her temples was like the blows of sledges.

Once, midway of the distance, as she stood lightly balanced, with arms outstretched, something went wrong with her equilibrium. She started forward as she had often done when a child, with the sensation of falling on her face. Her skirt billowed out in front of her. If she had had any breath in her, she would have cried out.

But the automatisms of her body worked better than her overtaxed brain. Her right foot went out easily and softly—she marvelled at that independent motion of her leg—and, taking up the falling weight of her body, restored her balance.

Mrs. Brace's voice had not faltered, although she must have seen the misstep. Arthur Sloane's bowed shoulders had not stirred. Mrs. Brace continued the printed enumeration of her stores of knowledge.

Lucille took another step. She was safe!—almost. There remained but a yard of her painful progress. One more step, she comforted herself, would put her on the threshold of the entry door, and from there to the corridor door, shielded by the entry wall from possible observation by her father, would be an easy business.

She completed that last step. On the threshold, she had to turn her body through an arc of ninety degrees, unless she backed out of the door. This she was afraid to do; her heel might meet an obstruction; a raised plank of the flooring, even, would mean an alarming noise.

She began to turn. The reading continued. The whole journey from door to door, in spite of the anguished care of every step, had consumed scarcely a minute. She was turning, the balancing arms outstretched. Deep down in her chest there was the beginning of a sensation, muscles relaxing, the promise of a long breath of relief.

Her left hand—or, perhaps, her elbow; in the blinding, benumbing flash of consternation, she did not know which—touched the pile of magazines on the table that was set against the door-frame. The magazines did not fall to the floor, but the fluttering of the loose cover of the one on top made a noise.

She fled, taking with her the flashing memory of the first stirring of her father's figure and the crackle of the paper in Mrs. Brace's hand. In two light steps she was at the corridor door. Her hands found the latch and turned it. She ran down the stairs with rapid, skimming steps, the door clicking softly shut as she made the turn on the next landing.

Her exit had been wonderfully quiet. She knew this, in spite of the fact that her straining senses had exaggerated the flutter of the magazine cover and the click of the door into a terrifying volume of sound. It was entirely possible that Mrs. Brace had been able to persuade her father that he had heard nothing more than some outside noise. She was certain that he had not seen her.

She crossed the dim, narrow lobby of the Walman so quickly, and so quietly, that the girl at the telephone board did not look in her direction.

Once in the street, she was seized by desire to confide to Hastings the story of her experience. She decided to act on the impulse.

He was at first more concerned with her physical condition than with what she had to tell. He saw how near she was to the breaking point.

"My dear child!" he said, in the tone of fatherly solicitude which she had learned to like. "Comfort before conference! Here, this chair by the window—so—and this wreck of a fan, can you use it? Fine! Now, cool your flushed face in this thin, very thin stream of a breeze—feel it? A glass of water?—just for the tinkling of ice? That's better, isn't it?"

The only light in the room was the reading lamp, under a dark-green shade, and from this little island of illumination there ran out a chaotic sea of shadows, huge waves of them, mounting the height of the book-shelves and breaking irregularly on the ceiling.

In the dimness, as he walked back and forth hunting for the fan or bringing her the water, he looked weirdly large—like, she thought dully, a fairy giant curiously draped. But the serenity of his expression touched her. She was glad she had come.

While she told her story, he stood in front of her, encouraging her with a smile or a nod now and then, or ambled with soft step among the shadows, always keeping his eyes upon her. For the moment, her tired spirit was freshened by his lavish praise of the manner in which she had accomplished her undertaking. Following that, his ready sympathy made it easier for her to discuss her fear that her father had planned to bribe Mrs. Brace.

Nevertheless, the effort taxed her severely. At the end of it, she leaned back and closed her eyes, only to open them with a start of fright at the resultant dizziness. The sensation of bodily lightness had left her. Her limbs felt sheathed in metal. An acute, throbbing pain racked her head. She was too weary to combat the depression which was like a cold, freezing hand at her heart.

"You don't say anything!" she complained weakly.

He stood near her chair, gazing thoughtfully before him.

"I'm trying to understand it," he said; "why your father did that. You're right, of course. He went there to pay her to keep quiet. But why?"

He looked at her closely.

"Could it be possible," he put the inquiry at last, "that he knew her before the murder?"

"I've asked him," she said. "No; he never had heard of her—neither he nor Judge Wilton. I even persuaded him to question Jarvis about that. It was the same; Jarvis never had—until last Sunday morning."

"You think of everything!" he congratulated her.

"No! Oh, no!"

Some quick and overmastering emotion broke down the last of her endurance. Whether it was a new and finer appreciation of his persistent, untiring search for the guilty man, or the realization of how sincerely he liked her, giving her credit for a frankness she had not exercised—whatever the pivotal consideration was, she felt that she could no longer deceive him.

She closed her lips tightly, to keep back the rising sobs, and regarded him with questioning, fearful eyes.

"What is it?" he asked gently, reading her appealing look.

"I've a confession to make," she said miserably.

He refused to treat it as a tragedy.

"But it can't be very bad!" he exclaimed pleasantly. "When we're overwrought, imagination's like a lantern swinging in the wind, changing the size of everything every second."

"But it is bad!" she insisted. "I haven't been fair. I couldn't bring myself to tell you this. I tried to think you'd get along without it!"

"And now?"

She answered him with an outward calmness which was, in reality, emotional dullness. She had suffered so much that to feel vividly was beyond her strength.

"You have the right to know it," she said, looking at him out of brilliant, unwinking eyes. "It's about father. He was out there—on the lawn—before he turned on the light in his room. I heard him come in, a minute before Berne went down the back stairs and out to the lawn. And I heard him go to his window and stand there, looking out, at least five long minutes before he flashed on his light."

He waited, thinking she might have more to tell. Construing his silence as reproof, she said, without changing either her expression or her voice:

"I know—it's awful. I should have told you. Perhaps, I've done great harm."

"You've been very brave," he consoled her, with infinite tenderness. "But it happens that I'd already satisfied myself on that point. I knew he'd been out there."

She was dumb, incapable of reacting to his words. Even the fact that he was smiling, with genuine amusement, did not affect her.

"Here comes the grotesque element, the comical, that's involved in so many tragedies," he explained. "Your father's weakness for 'cure' of nervousness, and his shrinking from the ridicule he's suffered because of it—there's the explanation of why he was out there that night."

She could not see significance in that, but neither could she summon energy to say so. She wondered vaguely why he thought it funny.

"That night—rather, the early morning hours following—while the rest of you were in the library, I looked through his room, and I found a pair of straw sandals in the closet—such as a man could slip on and off without having to bend down to adjust them. And they were wet, inside and out.

"Sunday morning, when Judge Wilton and I were at his bedside, I saw on the table a 'quack' pamphlet on the 'dew' treatment for nervousness, the benefit of the 'wet, cooling grass' upon the feet at night. You know the kind of thing. So—"

"Oh-h-h!" she breathed, tremulous and weak. "So that's why he was out there! Why didn't I think? Oh, how I've suspected him of—"

"But remember," he warned; "that's why he went out. We still don't know what he—what happened after he got out there—or why he's refused to say that he ever was out there. When we think of this, and other things, and, too, his call tonight on Mrs. Brace, for bribery—leaving what we thought was a sickbed—"

"But he's been up all day!" she corrected.

"And yet," he said, and stopped, reflecting.

"Tell me," she implored; "tell me, Mr. Hastings, do you suspect my father—or not—of the—?"

He answered her unfinished question with a solemn, painstaking care:

"Miss Sloane, you're not one who would want to be misled. You can bear the truth. I'd be foolish to say that he's not under suspicion. He is. Any one of the men there that night may have committed the murder. Webster, your father, Wilton—only there, suspicion seems totally gratuitous—Eugene Russell, Jarvis—I've heard things about him—any one of them may have struck that blow—may have."

"And father," she said, in a grieved bewilderment, "has paid Mrs. Brace to stop saying she suspects Berne," she shuddered, facing the alternative, "or himself!"

"You see," he framed the conclusion for her, "how hard he makes it for us to keep him out of trouble—if that gets out. He's put his hand on the live wire of circumstantial evidence, a wire that too often thrashes about, striking the wrong man."

"And Berne?" she cried out. "I think I could stand anything if only I knew—"

But this time the mutinous sobs came crowding past her lips. She could not finish the inquiry she had begun.

XVIII

The Man Who Rode Away

It was early in the afternoon of Wednesday when Mr. Hastings, responding to the prolonged ringing of his telephone, took the receiver off the hook and found himself in communication with the sheriff of Alexandria county. This was not the vacillating, veering sheriff who had spent nearly four days accepting the hints of a detective or sitting, chameleon-minded, at the feet of a designing woman. Here was an impressive and self-appreciative gentleman, one who delighted in his own deductive powers and relished their results.

He said so. His confidence fairly rattled the wire. His words annihilated space grandly and leaped into the old man's receptive ear with sizzling and electric effect. Mr. Crown, triumphant, was glad to inform others that he was making a hit with himself.

"Hello! That you, Hastings? Well, old fellow, I don't like to annoy you with an up-to-date rendition of 'I told you so!'—but it's come out, to the last syllable, exactly as I said it would—from the very first!"

Ensued a pause, for dramatic effect. The detective did not break it.

"Waiting, are you? Well, here she goes; Russell's alibi's been knocked into a thousand pieces! It's blown up! It's gone glimmering!—What do you think of that?"

Hastings refrained from replying that he had regarded such an event as highly probable. Instead, he inquired:

"And that simplifies things?"

"Does it!" exploded Mr. Crown. "I'm getting to you a few minutes ahead of the afternoon papers. You'll see it all there." An apologetic laugh came over the wire. "You'll excuse me, I know; I had to do this thing up right, put on the finishing touches before you even guessed what was going on. I've wound up the whole business. The Washington police nabbed Russell an hour ago, on my orders.

"'Simplifies things?' I should say so! I guess you can call 'em 'simplified' when a murder's been committed and the murderer's waiting to step into my little ring-tum-fi-diddle-dee of a country jail! 'No clue to this mystery,' the papers have been saying! What's the use of a clue when you *know* a guy's guilty? That's what I've been whistling all along!"

"But the alibi?" Hastings prompted. "You say it's blown up?"

"Blown! Gone! Result of my sending out those circulars asking if any automobile parties passed along the Sloanehurst road the murder night. Remember?"

"Yes." The old man recalled having made that suggestion, but did not say so.

"This morning the chief of police of York—York, Pennsylvania—wired me. I got him by long-distance right away. He gave me the story, details absolutely right and straight, all verified—and everything. A York man, named Stevens, saw a newspaper account, for the first time this morning, of the murder. He and four other fellows were in a car that went up Hub Hill that night a little after eleven—a few minutes after.—Hear that?"

"Yes. Go on."

"Stevens was on the back seat. They went up the hill on low—terrible piece of road, he calls it—they were no more than crawling. He says he was the only sober man in the crowd—been out on a jollification tour of ten days. He saw a man slide on to the running board on his side of the car as they were creeping up the hill. The rest of the party was singing, having a high old time.

"Stevens said he never said a word, just watched the guy on the running board, and planned to crack him on the head with an empty beer bottle when they got on the straight road and were hitting up a good clip—just playing, you understand.

"After he'd watched the guy a while and was trying to fish up a beer bottle from the bottom of the car, the chauffeur slowed down and hollered back to him on the back seat that he wanted to stop and look at his radiator—it was about to blow up, too hot. He'd been burning the dust on that stretch of good road.

"When he slowed down, the guy on the running board slipped off. Stevens says he rolled down a bank."

The jubilant Mr. Crown stopped, for breath.

"That's all right, far as it goes," Hastings said; "but does he identify that man as Russell?"

"To the last hair on his head!" replied the sheriff. "Stevens' description of the fellow is Russell all over—all over! Just to show you how good it is, take this: Stevens describe the clothes Russell wore, and says what Otis said: he'd lost his hat."

"Stevens got a good look at him?"

"Says the headlights were full on him as he stood on one side of the road, there on Hub Hill, waiting to slide on the running board.—And this Stevens is a shrewd guy, the York chief says. I guess his story plugs Russell's lies, shoots that alibi so full of holes it makes a sifter look like a piece of sheet-iron!

"That car went up Hub Hill at seven minutes past eleven—that means Russell had plenty of time to kill the girl after the rain stopped and to get out on the road and slip on to that running board. And the car slowed up, where he rolled off the running board, at eighteen minutes past eleven.

"Time's right, location's right, identification's right!—Pretty sweet, ain't it, old fellow? Congratulate me, don't you? Congratulate me, even if it does step on all those mysterious theories of yours—that right?"

Hastings bestowed the desired felicitations upon the exuberant conqueror of crime.

Turning from the telephone, he gazed a long time at the piece of grey envelope on the table before him. He had clung to his belief that, in those fragments of words, was to be found a clue to the solution of the mystery. He picked up his knife and fell to whittling.

Outside in the street a newsboy set up an abrupt, blaring din, shouting sensational headlines:

"SLOANEHURST MYSTERY SOLVED!—RUSSELL THE MURDERER!—ALIBI A FAKE!"

The old man considered grimly, the various effects of this development in the case—Lucille Sloane's unbounded relief mingled with censure of him for having added to her fears, and especially for having subjected her to the ordeal of last night's experience with Mrs. Brace—the adverse criticism from both press and public because of his refusal to join in the first attacks upon Russell, Arthur Sloane's complacency at never having treated him with common courtesy.

His thoughts went to Mrs. Brace and her blackmail schemes, as he had interpreted or suspected them.

"If I'd had a little more time," he reflected, "I might have put my hand on—"

His eyes rested on the envelope flap. His mind flashed to another and new idea. His muscles stiffened; he put his hands on the arms of his chair and slowly lifted himself up, the knife dropping from his fingers and clattering on the floor. He stood erect and held both hands aloft, a gesture of wide and growing wonder.

"Cripes!" he said aloud.

He picked up the grey paper with a hand that trembled. His pendent cheeks puffed out like those of a man blowing a horn. He stared at the paper again, before restoring it to its envelope, which he put back into one of his pockets.

"Cripes!" he said again. "It's a place! Pursuit! That's where the—"

He became a whirlwind of action, covered the floor with springy step. Taking a book of colossal size from a shelf, he whirled the pages, running his finger down a column while he murmured, "Pursuit—P-u-r—P-u—P-u—"

But there was no such name in the postal directory. He went back to older directories. He began to worry. Was there no such postoffice as Pursuit? He went to other books, whirling the pages, running down column after column. And at last he got the information he sought.

Consulting a railroad folder, he found a train schedule that caused him to look at his watch.

"Twenty-five minutes," he figured. "I'm going!"

He telephoned for a cab.

Then, seating himself at the table, he tore a sheet from a scratch-pad and wrote:

"Don't lose sight of Mrs. Brace. Disregard Russell's arrest.

"Hendricks: the Sloanehurst people are members of the Arlington Golf Club. Get a look at golf bags there. Did one, or two, contain piece or pieces of a bed-slat?

"Gore: check up on Mrs. B.'s use of money.

"I'll be back Sunday."

He sealed the envelope into which he put that, and, addressing it to Hendricks, left it lying on the table.

At the station he bought the afternoon newspapers and turned to Eugene Russell's statement, made to the reporters immediately after his arrest. It ran:

"I repeat that I'm innocent of the murder. Of course, I made a mistake in omitting all mention of my having ridden the first four miles from Sloanehurst. But, being innocent and knowing the weight of the circumstantial evidence against me, I could not resist the temptation to make my alibi good. I neither committed that murder nor witnessed it. The story I told at the inquest of what happened to me and what I did at Sloanehurst stands. It is the truth."

XIX

"Pursuit!"

Returning from his trip Sunday morning, the detective, after a brief conference with Hendricks, had gone immediately to Mrs. Brace's apartment. She sat now, still and watchful, on the armless rocker by the window, waiting for him to disclose the object of his visit. Except the lifted, faintly interrogating eyebrows, there was nothing in her face indicative of what she thought.

He caught himself comparing her to a statue, forever seated on the low-backed, uncomfortable chair, awaiting without emotion or alteration of feature the outcome of her evil scheming. Her hardness gave him the impression of something hammered on, beaten into an ugly pattern.

Having that imperturbability to overcome, he struck his first blow with surprising directness.

"I'm just back from Pursuit," he said.

That was the first speech by either of them since the monosyllabic greeting at the door. He saw that she had prepared herself for such an announcement; but the way she took it reminded him of a door shaken by the impact of a terrific blow. A little shiver, for all her force of repression, moved her from head to foot.

"You are?" she responded, her voice controlled, the hard face untouched by the shock to which her body had responded.

"Yes; I got back half an hour ago, and, except for one of my assistants, you're the first person I've seen." When that drew no comment from her, he added: "I want you to remember that—later on."

He began to whittle.

"Why?" she asked with genuine curiosity, after a pause.

"Because it may be well for you to know that I'm dealing with you alone, and fairly.—I got all the facts concerning you."

"Concerning me?" Her tone intimated doubt.

"Now, Mrs. Brace!" he exclaimed, disapproving her apparent intention. "You're surely not going to pretend ignorance—or innocence!"

She crossed her knees, and, putting her left forearm across her body, rested her right elbow in that hand. She began to rock very gently, her posture causing her to lean forward and giving her a look of continual but polite questioning.

"If you want to talk to me," she said, her voice free of all feeling, "you'll have to tell me what it's about."

"All right; I will," he returned. "You'll remember, I take it, my asking you to tell me the meaning of the marks on the flap of the grey envelope. I'll admit I was slow, criminally slow, in coming to the conclusion that 'Pursuit!' referred to a place rather than an act. But I got it finally—and I found Pursuit—not much left of it now; it's not even a postoffice.

"But it's discoverable," he continued on a sterner note, and began to shave long, slender chips from his block of wood. "I'll give you the high lights: young Dalton was killed—his murderer made a run for it—but you, a young widow then, in whose presence the thing was done, smoothed matters out. You swore it was a matter of self-defence. The result was that, after a few half-hearted attempts to locate the fugitive, the pursuit was given up."

"Very well. But why bring that story here—now? What's its significance?"

He stared at her in amazement. Her thin, sensitive lips were drawn back at the corners, enough to make her mouth look a trifle wider—and enough to suggest dimly that their motion was the start of a vindictive grimace. Otherwise, she was unmoved, unresponsive to the open threat of what he had said.

"Let me finish," he retorted. "An unfortunate feature, for you, was that you seemed to have made money out of the tragedy. In straitened circumstances previously, you began to spend freely—comparatively speaking—a few days after the murderer's disappearance. In fact, bribery was hinted; you had to leave the village. See any significance in that?" he concluded, with irony.

"Suppose you explain it," she said, still cool.

"The significance is in the strengthening of the theory I've had throughout the whole week that's passed since your daughter was killed at Sloanehurst."

"What's that?"

She stopped rocking; her eyes played a fiery tattoo on every feature of his face.

"Your daughter's death was the unexpected result of your attempts to blackmail young Dalton's murderer. You, being afraid of him, and not confessing that timidity to Mildred, persuaded her to approach him—in person."

"I! Afraid of him!" she objected, aroused at last.

Her brows were lowered, a heavy line above her furtive, swift eyes; her nostrils fluttered nervously.

"Granting your absurd theory," she continued, "why should I have feared him? What had he done—except strike to save his own life?"

"You forget, Mrs. Brace," he corrected. "That body showed twenty-nine wounds, twenty-eight of them unnecessary—if the first was inflicted in mere self-defence. It was horrible mutilation."

"So!" she ridiculed, with obvious effort. "You picture him as a butcher."

"Precisely. And you, having seen to what lengths his murderous fury could take him, were afraid to face him—even after your long, long search had located him again. Let's be sensible, Mrs. Brace. Let's give the facts of this business a hearing.

"You had come to Washington and located him at last. But, after receiving several demands from you, he'd stopped reading your letters—sent them back unopened. Consequently, in order for you to make an appointment with him, he had to be communicated with in a handwriting he didn't know. Hence, your daughter had to write the letter making that appointment a week ago last night. Then, however—"

"What makes you think—"

"Then, however," he concluded, overbearing her with his voice, "you hadn't the courage to face him—out there, in the dark, alone. You persuaded Mildred to go—in your place. And he killed her."

"Ha!" The mocking exclamation sounded as though it had been pounded out of her by a blow upon her back. "What makes you say that? Where do you get that? Who put that into your head?"

She volleyed those questions at him with indescribable rapidity, her lips drawn back from her teeth, her brows straining far up toward the line of her hair. The profound disgust with which he viewed her did not affect her. She darted to and fro in her mind, running about in the waste and tumult of her momentary confusion, seeking the best thing to say, the best policy to adopt, for her own ends.

He had had time to determine that much when her gift of self-possession reasserted itself. She forced her lips back to their thin line, and steadied herself. He could see the vibrant tautness of her whole body, exemplified in the rigidity with which she held her crossed knees, one crushed upon the other.

"I know, I think, what misled you," she answered her own question. "You've talked to Gene Russell, of course. He may have heard—I think he did hear—Mildred and me discussing the mailing of a letter that Friday night."

"He did," Hastings said, firmly.

"But he couldn't have heard anything to warrant your theory, Mr. Hastings. I merely made fun of her wavering after she'd once said she'd confront Berne Webster again with her appeal for fair play."

He inspected her with an emotion that was a mingling of incredulity and repugnant wonder.

"It's no use, Mrs. Brace," he told her. "Russell didn't see the name of the man to whom the letter was addressed. I saw him last Sunday afternoon. He told me he took the name for granted, because Mildred had taunted him, saying it went to Webster. As a matter of fact, he wanted to see if Webster was at Sloanehurst and fastened his eyes for a fleeting glimpse on that word—and on that alone. Besides, there are facts to prove that the letter did not go to Webster.—Do you see how your fancied security falls away?"

"Let me think," she said, her tone flat and impersonal.

She was silent, her restless eyes gazing at the wall over his head. He watched her, and glanced only at intervals at the wood he was aimlessly shaving.

"Of course," she said, after a while, looking at him with a speculative, deliberating air, "you've deduced and pieced this together. You've a woman's intuition—comprehension of motives, feelings."

She was silent again.

"Pieced what together?" he asked.

"It's plain enough, isn't it? You began with your suspicion that my need of money was heavier in my mind than grief at Mildred's death. On that, you built up—well, all you've just said."

"It was more than a suspicion," he corrected. "It was knowledge—that everything you did, after her death, was intended to help along your scheme to—we'll say, to get money."

"Still," she persisted shrewdly, "you felt the necessity of proving I'd blackmail—if that's the word you want to use."

"How?" he put in quickly. "Prove it, how?"

"That's why you sent that girl here with the five hundred. I see it now; although, at the time, I didn't." She laughed, a short, bitter note. "Perhaps, the money, or my need of it, kept me from thinking straight."

"Well?"

"Of course," she made the admission calmly, "as soon as I took the hush money, your theory seemed sound—the whole of it: my motives and identity of the murderer."

She was thinking with a concentration so intense that the signs of it resembled physical exertion. Moisture beaded the upper part of her forehead. He could see the muscles of her face respond to the locking of her jaws.

"But there's nothing against me," she began again, and, moved by his expression, qualified: "nothing that I can be held for, in the courts."

"You've decided that, have you?"

"You'll admit it," she said. "There's nothing—there can be nothing—to disprove my statement that Dalton's death was provoked. I hold the key to that—I alone. That being true, I couldn't be prosecuted in Pursuit as 'accessory after the fact.'"

"Yes," he agreed. "That's true."

"And here," she concluded, without a hint of triumph, even without a special show of interest, "I can't be proceeded against for blackmail. That money, from both of them, was a gift. I hadn't asked for it, much less demanded it. I," she said with an assured arrogance, "hadn't got that far.—So, you see, Mr. Hastings, I'm far from frightened."

He found nothing to say to that shameless but unassailable declaration. Also, he was aware that she entertained, and sought solution of, a problem, the question of how best to satisfy her implacable determination to make the man pay. That purpose occupied all her mind, now that her money greed was frustrated.

It was on this that he had calculated. It explained his going to her before confronting the murderer. He had felt certain that her perverted desire to "get even" would force her into the strange position of helping him.

He broke the silence with a careful attempt to guide her thoughts:

"But don't fool yourself, Mrs. Brace. You've got out of this all you'll ever get, financially—every cent. And you're in an unpleasant situation— an outcast, perhaps. People don't stand for your line of stuff, your behaviour."

She did not resent that. Making a desperate mental search for the best way to serve her hard self-interest, he thought, she was impervious to insult.

"I know," she said, to his immense relief. "I've been considering the only remaining point."

"What's that?"

"The sure way to make him suffer as horribly as possible."

He pretended absorption in his carving.

"Why shouldn't he have provided me with money when I asked it?" she demanded, at last.

The new quality of her speech brought his head up with a jerk. Instead of colourless harshness, it had a warm fury. It was not that she spoke loudly or on a high key; but it had an unbridled, self-indulgent sound. He got the impression that she put off all censorship from either her feeling or her expression.

"That wasn't much to ask—as long as he continued his life of ease, of luxury, of safety—as long as I left out of consideration the debt he couldn't pay, the debt that was impossible of payment."

Alien as the thing seemed in connection with her, he grasped it. She thought that she had once loved the man.

"The matter of personal feeling?" he asked.

"Yes. When he left Pursuit, he destroyed the better part of me—what you would call the good part."

She said that without sentimentalism, without making it a plea for sympathy; she had better sense, he saw, than to imagine that she could arouse sympathy on that ground.

"And," she continued, with intense malignity, "what was so monstrous in my asking him for money? I asked him for no payment of what he really owes me. That's a debt he can't pay! My beauty, destroyed, withered and covered over with the hard mask of the features you see now; my capacity for happiness, dead, swallowed up in my long, long devotion to my purpose to find him again—those things, man as you are, you realize are beyond the scope of payment or repayment!"

Without rising to a standing position, she leaned so far forward that her weight was all on her feet, and, although her figure retained the posture of one seated on a chair, she was in fact independent of support from it, and held herself crouching in front of him, taut, a tremor in her limbs because of the strain.

Her hands were held out toward him, the tips of her stiffened, half-closed fingers less than a foot from his face. Her brows were drawn so high that the skin of her forehead twitched, as if pulled upward by another's hand. It was with difficulty that he compelled himself to witness the climax of her rage. Only his need of what she knew kept him still.

"Money!" she said, her lean arms in continual motion before him. "You're right, there. I wanted money. I made up my mind I'd have it. It was such a purpose of mine, so strongly grown into my whole being, that even Mildred's death couldn't lessen or dislodge it. And there was more than the want of money in my never letting loose of my intention to find him. He couldn't strip me bare and get away! You've understood me pretty well. You know it was written, on the books, that he and I should come together again—no matter how far he went, or how cleverly!

"And I see now!" she gave him her decision, and, as she did so, rose to an upright position, her hands at her sides going half-shut and open, half-shut and open, as if she made mental pictures of the closing in of her long pursuit. "I'll say what you want me to say. Confront him; put me face to face with him, and I'll say the letter went to him. Oh, never fear! I'll say the appropriate thing, and the convincing thing—appropriately convincing!"

Her eyes glittered, countering his searching glance, as she stood over him, her body flung a little forward from the waist, her arms busy with their quick, angular gesticulation.

"When?" he asked. "When will you do that?"

"Now," she answered instantly. "Now!—Now!—Oh, don't look surprised. I've thought of this possibility. My God!" she said with a bitterness that startled him. "I've thought of every possibility, every possible crook and quirk of this business."

She was struck by his slowness in responding to her offer.

"But you," she asked; "are you sure—have you the proof?"

"Thanks," he said drily. "You needn't be uneasy about that.—Now, if I may do a little telephoning, we'll start."

He went a step from her and turned back.

"By the way," he stipulated, "that little matter of the five hundred—you needn't refer to it. I mean it will have to be left out. It's not necessary."

"No; it isn't," she agreed, with perfect indifference. "And it's spent."

When he had telephoned to Sloanehurst and the sheriff's office, he found her with her hat on, ready to accompany him.

As they stepped out of the Walman, she saw the automobile waiting for them. She stopped, a new rage darting from her eyes. He thought she would go back. After a brief hesitation, however, she gave a short, ugly laugh.

"You were as sure as that, were you!" she belittled herself. "Had the car wait—to take me there!"

"By no means," he denied. "I hoped you'd go—that's all."

"That's better," she said, determined to assert her individuality of action. "You're not forcing me into this, you know. I'm doing it, after thinking it out to the last detail—for my own satisfaction."

XX

Denial of the Charge

Hastings, fully appreciating the value of surprise, had instructed Mrs. Brace to communicate none of the new developments to anybody until he asked for them. Reaching Sloanehurst, he went alone to the library, leaving her in the parlour to battle as best she might with the sheriff's anxious curiosity.

Arthur Sloane and Judge Wilton gave him cool welcome, parading for his benefit an obvious and insolent boredom. Although uninvited to sit down, he caught up a chair and swung it lightly into such position that, when he seated himself, he faced them across the table. He was smiling, enough to indicate a general satisfaction with the world.

There was in his bearing, however, that which carried them back to their midnight session with him immediately following the discovery of Mildred Brace's body. The smile did not lessen his look of unquestionable power; his words were sharp, clipped-off.

"I take it," he said briskly, untouched by their demeanour of indifference, "you gentlemen will be interested in the fact that I've cleared up this mystery."

"Ah-h-h!" drawled Sloane. "Again?"

"What do you mean by 'again'?" he asked, good-naturedly.

"Crown, the sheriff, accomplished it four days ago, I'm credibly informed."

"He made a mistake."

"Ah?" Sloane ridiculed.

"Yes. 'Ah!'" Hastings took him up curtly, and, with a quick turn of his head, addressed himself to Wilton: "Judge, I've been to Pursuit."

When he said that, his head was thrown back so that he squinted at Wilton down the line of his nose, under the rims of his spectacles.

"Pursuit!"

Wilton's echo of the word was explosive. He had been leaning back in his chair, eying the detective from under lowered lids, and drawing deep, prolonged puffs from his cigar. But, with the response to Hastings' announcement, he sat up and leaned forward, putting his elbows on the rim of the table. It was an awkward attitude, compelling him to extend his neck and turn his face upward in order to meet the other's glance.

"Yes," Hastings said, after a measurable pause. "Interested in that?"

"Not at all," Wilton replied, plainly alarmed, and fubbed out his cigar with forefinger and thumb, oblivious to the fact that he dropped a little shower of fire on the table cover.

"I'll trouble you to observe, Mr. Sloane," Hastings put in, "that, being excited, the judge's first impulse is to extinguish his cigar: it's a habit of his.—Now, judge, in Pursuit I heard a lot about you—a lot."

"All right—what?"

He made the inquiry reluctantly, as if under compulsion of the detective's glance.

"The Dalton case—and your part in it."

"You know about that, do you?"

"All about it," Hastings said, in a way that made doubt impossible; Sloane, even, bewildered as he was, got the impression of his ruthless certainty.

Wilton did not contest it.

"I struck in self-defence," he excused himself wearily, like a man taking up a task against his will. "It would be ridiculous to call that murder. No jury would have convicted me—none would now, if given the truth."

"But the body showed twenty-nine wounds," Hastings pressed him, "the marks of twenty-nine separate thrusts of that knife."

"Yes; that's true.—Yes, I'll tell you about that, you and Arthur—if you'd care to hear?"

"That's what I'm here for," Hastings said, settling in his chair. He was thinking: "He didn't expect this. He's unprepared!"

Sloane, who had been on the point of resenting this unbelievable attack on his friend, was struck dumb by Wilton's calm acknowledgment of the charge. From long habit, he took the cap off the smelling-salts with which he had been toying when Hastings came in, but his shaking hand could not lift the bottle to his nose. Wilton guilty of a murder, years ago! He drew a long, shuddering breath and huddled in his chair.

Wilton rose clumsily and walked heavily to the door opening into the hall. He put his hand on the knob but did not turn it. He repeated the performance at the door opening into Sloane's room. In all this he was unconscionably slow, moving in the manner of a blind man, feeling his way about and fumbling both knobs.

When he came back to the table, his shoulders were hunched to the front and downward, crowding his chest. His face looked larger, each separate feature of it throbbing coarsely to the pumping of his heart. Pink threads stood out on the white of his eyeballs. When the back of his neck pressed against his collar, the effect was to give the lower half of the back of his head an odd appearance of inflation or puffiness.

Hastings had never seen a man struggle so to contain himself.

"Suffering angels!" Sloane sympathized shrilly. "What's the matter, Tom?"

"All right—it's all right," he assured, his voice still low, but so resonant and harsh that it sounded like the thrumming of a viol string.

He seated himself, moving his chair several times, adjusting it to a proper angle to the table. In the end, he sat close to the table rim, hunched heavily on his elbows, and looked straight at Hastings.

"But, since you've been to Pursuit, what do you imply, or say?" he asked, the words scraping, as though his throat had been roughened with a file.

"That you killed Mildred Brace," Hastings answered, also leaning forward, to give the accusation weight.

"I! I killed her!" Wilton's teeth went together with a sharp click; the table sagged under his weight. "I deny it. I deny it!" He ripped out an oath. "This man's crazy, Arthur! He's dragged up a mistake, a tragedy, of my youth, and now has the effrontery to use it as a reason for suspecting me of murder!"

"Exactly!" chimed Sloane, in tremulous relief. "Shivering saints! Why haven't you said so long ago, Tom?"

"I didn't give him credit for the wild insanity he's showing," said Wilton thickly.

Whatever had been his first impulse, however near he had been to trying to explain away all blame in the Dalton murder, it was clear to Hastings now that he intended to rely on flat denial of his connection with the death of Mildred Brace. He had, perhaps, decided that explanation was too difficult.

Seeing his indecision, Hastings turned on Sloane.

"You've been exceedingly offensive to me on several occasions, Mr. Sloane. And I've had enough of it. Now, I've got the facts to show that you're as foolish in the selection of your friends as in making enemies. I'm about to charge this man Wilton with murder. He killed Mildred Brace, and I can prove it. If you want to hear the facts back of this mystery; if you want the stuff that will enable you to decide whether you'll stand by him or against him, you can have it!"

Before Sloane could recover from his surprise at the old man's hot resentment, Wilton said, with an air of careless contempt:

"Oh, we've got to deal with what he says, Arthur. I'd rather answer it here than with an audience."

"The reading public, for instance?" Hastings retorted, and added: "It may interest you, Mr. Sloane, to know that you gave me my first suspicion of him. When you stepped back from the handkerchief I held out to you—remember, as I was kneeling over the body, and the servant laughed at you?—I jammed it into Wilton's right-hand coat-pocket.

"Later, when I got it back from him, I saw clinging to it a few cigar ashes and two small particles of wet tobacco. He had had in that pocket a cigar stump wet from his saliva.

"When he began then his story of finding the body, he said, 'I'd been smoking my good-night cigar; this is what's left of it.' As he said that, he pointed to the unlit—remember that, unlit—cigar stump between his teeth. He made it a point to emphasize the fact that so little time had elapsed between his finding the body and his giving the alarm that he hadn't smoked up the cigar, and also he hadn't taken time to put his hand to his mouth, take out the cigar and throw it away.

"It was one of the over-fine little touches that a guilty man tries to pile on his scheme for appearing innocent. But what are the facts?

"Just now, as soon as he got excited, he mechanically fubbed out his cigar. It's a habit of his—whenever he's in a close corner. He did it during the interview I had with him and Webster in the music room last Sunday morning—when, in fact, something dangerous to him came up. He did it again when I was talking to him in his office, following a visit from Mrs. Brace.

"There you have the beginning of my suspicion. Why had he gone out of his way to put a cigar stump into his pocket that night, and to explain that he had had it in his mouth all the time? When he came into my room, to wake me up, he had no cigar in his mouth. But, when you and I rounded the corner of the porch and first saw him kneeling over the body, he had one hand in his right-hand coat-pocket. And, when we stood beside him, he had put a half-smoked, unlit cigar into his mouth.

"You see my point, clearly? Instead of having had the cigar in his mouth and having kept it there while he found the body and reported the discovery to us, the truth is this: he had fubbed out the cigar when he met Mildred Brace on the lawn, and it had occurred to his calculating mind that it would be well, when he chose to give the alarm, to use the cigar stunt as evidence that he hadn't been engaged in quarrelling with and murdering a woman.

"He was right in his opinion that the average man doesn't go on calmly smoking while engaged in such activities. He was wrong in letting us discover where he'd carried the stump until he needed it.

"He had put it into that pocket, but, after committing the murder, he wasn't quite as calm as he'd expected to be—something had gone wrong; Webster had appeared on the scene—and the cigar wasn't restored to his mouth until you and I first reached the body.

"Here's my handkerchief, showing the ashes and the pieces of cigar tobacco on it, just as it was when he handed it back to me."

He took from one of his pockets a tissue-paper parcel, and, unwrapping it, handed it to Sloane.

"Ah-h-h-that's what it shows," Sloane admitted, bending over the handkerchief.

Wilton welcomed that with a laugh which he meant to be lightly contemptuous.

"See here, Arthur!" he objected. "I'm perfectly willing to listen to any sane statement this man may make, but—"

"You said you wanted to hear this!" Hasting stopped him. "I'm fair about it. I've told you why I began to watch you. I've got more."

"You need it," Sloane complained. "If it's all that thin—"

"Don't shout too soon," Hastings interrupted again. "Mr. Sloane, this man's been working against me from the start. Think a moment, and you'll realize it. While he was telling your daughter and a whole lot of other people that I was the only man to handle the case, he was slipping you the quiet instruction to avoid me, not to confide in me, not to tell me a single thing. Isn't that true?"

"We-ell, he did say the best way for me to avoid all possibility of being involved in the thing was not to talk to anybody."

"I knew it!" Hastings declared, giving his contempt full play. "And he persuaded you that you might have seen—*might*, mind you—and he gave you the suggestion skilfully, more by indirection than by flat statement— that you might have seen Berne Webster out there on the lawn that night, when you were uncertain, when you feared it yourself—a little. Isn't that true?"

Sloane looked at him with widening eyes, his lips trembling.

"Come, Mr. Sloane! Let's play fair, didn't he?"

"We-ell, yes."

"And," Hastings continued, thumping the table with a heavy hand to drive home the points of his statement, "he persuaded you to offer that money to Mrs. Brace—last Tuesday night.—Didn't he?—And that matches his slippery cunning in pretending he was saving Webster by hiding the fact that Webster's hand had gagged him when they found the body. He figured his willingness to help somebody else would keep suspicion away from him. I—"

"Rot! All rot!" Wilton broke in. "Where do you think you are, Arthur, on the witness stand? He'll have you saying white's black in a minute."

"Mr. Sloane," the detective said, getting to his feet, "he induced you to pay money to Mrs. Brace—while it's the colour of blackmail, it won't be a matter for prosecution; you gave it to her, in a sense, unsolicited—but he induced you to do that because he knew she was out for blackmail. He hoped that, if you bought her off, she wouldn't pursue him farther."

"Farther!" echoed Sloane. "What do you mean by that?"

"Why, man! Don't you see? Money was back of all that tragedy. He murdered the girl because she had come here to renew her mother's attempts at blackmail on him! Not content with duping you, with handling you as if you'd been a baby, he put you up to buying off the woman who was after him—and he did it by fooling you into thinking that you were saving the name, if not the very life, of your daughter's fiancé! He—"

"Lies! Wild lie!" thundered Wilton, pushing back from the table. "I'm through with—"

"No! No!" shrilled Sloane. "Wait! Prove that, Hastings! Prove it—if you can! Shuddering saints! Have I—?"

He looked once at Wilton's contorted face, and recoiled, the movement confessing at last his lack of faith in the man.

"I will," Hastings answered him, and moved toward the door; "I'll prove it—by the girl's mother."

He threw open the door, and, sure now of holding Sloane's attention, went in search of Mrs. Brace and the sheriff.

XXI

"Ample Evidence"

The two men in the library waited a long time for his return. Wilton, elbows on the table, stared straight in front of him, giving no sign of knowledge of the other's presence. Sloane fidgeted with the smelling-salts, emitting now and then long-drawn, tremulous sighs that were his own special vocabulary of dissatisfaction. He spoke once.

"Mute and cringing martyrs!" he said, in suspicious remonstrance. "If he'd say something we could deny! So far, Tom, you're mixed up in—"

"Why can't you wait until he's through?" Wilton objected roughly.

They heard people coming down the hall. Lucille, following Mrs. Brace into the room, went to her father. They could see, from her look of grieved wonder, that Hastings had told her of the charge against Wilton. The sheriff's expression confirmed the supposition. His mouth hung open, so that the unsteady fingers with which he plucked at his knuckle like chin appeared also to support his fallen jaw. He made a weak-kneed progress from the door to a chair near the screened fireplace.

For a full half-minute Hastings was silent, as if to let the doubts and suspense of each member of the group emphasize his dominance of the situation. He reviewed swiftly some of the little things he had used to build up in his own mind the certainty of Wilton's guilt: the man's agitation in the music room at the discovery, not that a part of the grey envelope had been found, but that it contained some of the words of the letter—his obvious alarm when found quarrelling with Mrs. Brace in his office—his hardly controlled impulses: once, outside Sloane's bedroom, to accuse Berne Webster without proof, and, on the Sloanehurst porch last Sunday, to suggest that Sloane was guilty.

The detective observed now that he absolutely ignored Mrs. Brace, not even looking in her direction. He perceived also how she reacted to that assumed indifference. The tightening of her lips, the flutter of her mobile nostrils, left him no longer any doubt that she was in the mood to give him the cooperation she had so bitterly promised.

"To be dragged down by such a woman!" he thought.

"Mrs. Brace," he said, "I've charged Judge Wilton with the murder of your daughter. I say now he killed her, with premeditation, having planned it after receiving a letter from her."

"Yes?" she responded, a certain tenseness in her voice.

She had gone to a chair by the window; and, like the sheriff, she faced the trio at the table: Wilton, Sloane, and Lucille, who stood behind her father, a hand on his shoulder.

Hastings slowly paced the floor as he talked, his hands clasped behind him and now and then moving the tail of his coat up and down. He glanced at Mrs. Brace over the rims of his spectacles, his eyes shrewd and keen. He showed an unmistakable self-satisfaction, like the elation Wilton had detected in his bearing on two former occasions.

"Now," he asked her, "what can you tell us about that letter?"

Wilton, his chest pressed so hard against the edge of the table that his breathing moved his body, turned his swollen face upon her at last, his eyes flaming under the thatch of his down-drawn brows.

Mrs. Brace, her high-shouldered, lean frame silhouetted against the window, began, in a colourless, unemotioned tone:

"As you know, Mr. Hastings, I thought this man Wilton owed me money, more than money. I'd looked for him for twenty-six years. Less than a year ago I located him here in Virginia, and I came to Washington. He refused my requests. Then, he stopped reading my letters—sent them back unopened at first; later, he destroyed them unread, I suppose."

She cleared her throat lightly, and spoke more rapidly. The intensity of her hate, in spite of her power of suppression, held them in a disagreeable fascination.

"I was afraid of him, afraid to confront him alone. I'd seen him kill a man. But I was in desperate need. I thought, if my daughter could talk to him, he would be brought to do the right thing. I suppose," she said with a wintry smile, "you'd call it an attempt to blackmail—if he had let it go far enough.

"She wrote him a letter, on grey paper, and sent it, in an oblong, grey envelope, to him here at Sloanehurst last Friday night. He got it Saturday afternoon. If he hadn't received it, he'd never have been out on the lawn—with a dagger he'd made for the occasion—at eleven or eleven-fifteen, which was the time Mildred said in her letter she'd see him there. She had added that, if he did not keep the appointment, she'd expose him—his crime in Pursuit."

"I see," Hastings said, on the end of her cold, metallic utterance, and took from his pocket the flap of grey envelope. "Is this the flap of that envelope; or, better still, are these fragments of words and the word 'Pursuit' in your daughter's handwriting?"

"I've examined them already," she said. "They are my daughter's writing."

Her lips were suddenly thick, taking on that appearance of abnormal wetness which had so revolted him before.

"And I say what you've just said!" she supplemented, her eyebrows high upon her forehead. "Tom Wilton killed my daughter. And, when I went to his office—I was sure then that he'd be afraid to harm me so soon after Mildred's death—I accused him of the murder. He took it with a laugh. He said I could look at it as a warning that—"

"Wait!"

The interruption came from Wilton.

"I'm going to make a statement about this thing!" he ground out, his voice coarse and rasping.

Hastings hung upon him with relentless gaze.

"What have you got to say?"

"Much!" returned Wilton. "I'm not going to let myself be ruined on this charge because of a mistake of my youth—mistake, I say! I'm about to tell you the story of such suffering, such misfortune, as no man has ever had to endure. It explains that tragedy in Pursuit; it explains my life; it explains everything. I didn't murder that boy Dalton. I struck in self-defence. But the twenty-nine wounds on his body—"

He paused, preoccupied; he was thinking less of his hearers than of himself. It was at that point, Hastings thought afterwards, that he began to lose himself in the ugly enjoyment of describing his cruelty. It was as if the horrors to which he gave voice subjected him to a specious and irresistible charm, equipped him with a spurious courage, a sincere indifference to common opinion.

"There is," he said, "a shadow on my soul. My greatest enemy is hidden in my own mind.

"But I've fought it, fought it all my life. You may say the makeshifts I've adopted, the strategy of my resistance, my tactics to outwit this thing, do me little credit. I shall leave it to you to decide. Results speak for themselves. I have broken no law; there is against me nothing that would bring upon me the penalty of man's laws."

He wedged himself more closely against the edge of the table, and struck his left palm with his clenched right hand.

"I tell you, Hastings, to have fought this thing, in whatever way, has been a task that called for every ounce of strength I had. I've lived in hell and walked with devils, against my will. Not a day, not a night, have I been free of this curse, or my fear of it. There have been times when, every night for months, my slumbers were broken or impossible! The devilish thing reached down into the depths of sleep and with its foul and muddy grasp poisoned even those clear, white pools—clear and white for other men! But no matter—

"You've heard of obsessions—of men seized every six months with an irresistible desire to drink—of kleptomaniacs who, having all they need or wish, must steal or go mad—of others driven by inexplicable impulse, mania, to set fire to buildings, for the thrill they get out of seeing the flames burst forth. Well, from my earliest childhood until that moment when Roy Dalton attacked me, I had fought an impulse even more terrible than those. God, what a tyranny! It drove me, drove me, that obsession, at times amounting to mental compulsion, to strike, to stab, to make the blood flow!"

He rose, getting to his feet slowly, so that his burly bulk gained in size, like the slow upheaval of a hillside. Swollen as his face had been, it expanded now a trifle more. His nostrils coarsened more perceptibly. The puffiness that had been in the back of his neck extended entirely around his throat. He hung forward over the table, giving all his attention to Hastings, who was unmoved, incredulous.

"The Brace woman will tell you I had to kill him," he proceeded more swiftly, displaying a questionable ardour, like a man foreseeing defeat. "The mistake I made was in running away—a bitter mistake! But those unnecessary wounds, twenty-eight that need not have been made! The obsession to see the blood flow drove me to acts which a jury, I thought, would not understand. And, if you don't see the force of my explanation, Hastings, if you don't understand, I shall be in little better plight—after all these years!"

He put, there, a sorrowful appeal into his voice; but a sly contradiction of it showed faintly in his face, a hint that he took a crafty pleasure in dragging into the light the depravity he had kept in darkness for a lifetime.

"I got away. I drifted to Virginia, working hard, studying much. I became a lawyer. But always I had that affliction to combat; all my life, man!—always! There were periods months long when devils came up from the ugly corners of my soul to torture and tempt me.

"It wasn't the ordinary temptation, not a weak, pale idea of 'I'd like to kill and see the blood!'—but an uproar, an imperial voice, an endless command: 'Kill! Draw blood! Kill!'—What it did to me—

"But to this day I've beaten it! I've been a good citizen. I've observed the law. I've refused to let that involuntary lust for blood ruin me or cast me out.

"Let me tell you how. I decided that, if I had a hand in awarding just punishments, my affliction would be abated enough for me to live in some measure of security. There you have the explanation of my being on the bench. I cheated the obsession to murder by helping to imprison or execute those who did murder!

"That's why I can tell you of my innocence of the Brace murder. Do you think I'd tell it unless I knew there could be not even an excuse for suspecting me? On the other hand, if I had kept silent as to the true motive that drove my hand to those unnecessary mutilations of young Dalton—the only time, remember, that my weakness ever got the better, or the worse, of me!—if I had kept silent on that, you would have had ground for suspecting me of a barbarous murder then, and, arguing from that, of the Brace murder now.

"Do I make myself clear?—Do you want me to go into further detail?"

He sank slowly back to his chair, spent by the strain of supreme effort. His breathing was laboured, stertorous.

"That, Crown," Hastings denounced, "is a confession! Knowing he's caught, he's got the insolence to whine for mercy because of his 'sufferings'! Think of it! The thing of which he boasts is the thing for which he deserves death—since death is supposed to be the supreme punishment. He tells us, in self-congratulatory terms, that he curbed his inhuman longings, satisfied his lust for blood, by going on the bench and helping to 'punish those who did murder!'

"Too cowardly to strike a blow, he skulked behind the protection of his position. He made of the judicial robe an assassin's disguise. On the bench, he was free to sate his thirst for others' sufferings—adding to a sentence five undeserved years here, ten there; slipping into his instructions to juries a phrase that would mean the death penalty!

"He revelled in judicial murders. He gloated over the helpless people who, looking to him for justice, were merely the victims of his abhorrent cruelty. He loved the look of sick surprise in their starting eyes. He got a filthy joy out of seeing a man turn pale. He rubbed his hands in glee when a woman swooned. He—"

"I can't stand that—can't stand it!" Sloane protested, hands over his eyes.

"What more do you want, to prove his guilt, his abominable guilt?" Hastings swept on. "You have the motive, hatred of this woman here and her daughter—you have the proof of the letter sent to him making the compulsory appointment—you have his own crazy explanation of his homicidal impulse, from which, by the way, he never sought relief, a queer 'impulse' since it gave him time, hours, to plan the crime and manufacture the weapon with which he killed!"

"I said at the start," Wilton put in hoarsely, "this man Hastings was only theorizing. If he had anything to connect me with—"

"I have!" Hastings told him, and came to a standstill in front of the sheriff, bending over him, as if to drive each statement into Crown's reluctant mind.

"He got that letter a little after five in the afternoon. He left me here, in this room, with Sloane and Webster, and was gone three-quarters of an hour. That was just before dinner. He had the second floor, on that side of the house, entirely to himself. He took a nail-file from Webster's dressing case, and in Webster's room put a sharper point on it by filing it roughly with the file-blade of his own pen knife.

"That's doubly proved: first, my magnet, with which I went over the floor in Webster's room, picked up small particles of steel. Here they are."

He produced a small packet and, without unwrapping it, handed it to Crown.

"Again: you'll find that the file-blade of his knife retained particles of the steel in the little furrows of its corrugated surface. I know, because last Sunday, as your car came up the driveway, I borrowed his knife, on the pretext of tightening a screw in the blade of mine. And I examined it."

He put up a silencing hand as Wilton forced a jeering laugh.

"But there's more to prove his manufacture and ownership of the weapon that killed the woman. He made the handle from the end of a slat on the bed in the room which I occupied that night. The inference is obvious: he didn't care to risk going outside the house to hunt for the wood he needed; he wouldn't take it from an easily visible place; and, having stolen something from one room, he paid his attention to mine. All this is the supercaution of the so-called 'smart criminal.' It matches the risk he took in returning to the body to hunt for the weapon. That was why he was there when Webster found the body.

"The handle of the dagger matches the wood of the slat I've just mentioned. You won't find that particular slat upstairs now. It was taken out of the house the next day, broken into sections and packed in his bag of golf-sticks. But there is proof in this room of the fact that he and he only made the dagger.

"You'll find in the edge of the large blade of his penknife a nick, triangular in shape, which left an unmistakable groove in the wood every time he cut into it. That little groove shows, to the naked eye, on the end of the shortened slat and on the handle of the dagger. If you doubt it—"

"Thunder!" Crown interrupted, in an awed tone. "You're right!"

He had taken the dagger from his pocket and given it minute scrutiny. He handed it now to Sloane.

Wilton, watching the scene with flaming eyes, sat motionless, his chin thrust down hard upon his collar, his face shining as if it had been polished with a cloth.

Sloane gave the dagger back to Crown before he spoke, in a wheezy, shrill key: "They're there, the marks, the grooves!"

He did not look at Wilton.

Hastings straightened to his full stature, and looked toward Wilton.

"Now, Judge Wilton," he challenged, "you said you preferred to answer the accusation here and now. Do you, still?"

Wilton, slowly raising the heavy lids of his eyes, like a man coming out of a trance, presented to him and to the others a face which, in spite of its flushed and swollen aspect, looked singularly bleak.

"It's not an accusation," he said in his roughened, grating voice. "It's a network of suppositions, of theories, of impossibilities—a crazy structure, all built on the rotten foundation of a previous misfortune."

"Arrest him, Crown!" Hastings commanded sharply.

Wilton tried to laugh, but his heavy lips merely worked in a crazy barrenness of sound. With a vague, clumsy idea of covering up his confusion, he started to light a cigar.

He stopped, hands in mid-air, when Crown, shambling to his feet, said:

"Judge, I've got to act. He's proved his case."

"Proved it!" Wilton made weak protest.

"If he hasn't, let's see your penknife."

Wilton put his hand into his trousers pocket, began the motion that would have drawn out the knife, checked it, and withdrew his hand empty. He managed a mirthless, dreary laugh, a rattling sound that fell, dead of any feeling, from his grimacing lips.

"No, by God!" he refused. "I'll give it to neither of you. I don't have to!"

In that moment, he fell to pieces. With his thick shoulders dropping forward, he became an inert mass bundled against the table edge. The blood went out of his face, so that his cheeks hollowed, and shadows formed under his eyes. He was like the victim of a quick consumption.

Crown's eyes were on Hastings.

"That's enough," the old man said shortly.

"Too much," agreed Crown. "Judge, there's no bail—on a murder charge."

"I'm very glad," Mrs. Brace commented, a terrible satisfaction in her voice. "He pays me—at last."

In the music room Dr. Garnet had just given Lucille and Hastings a favourable report on Berne Webster's condition.

"I should so like to tell him," she said, her glance entreating; "if you'll let me! Wouldn't he get well much faster if he knew it—knew the suspense was all over—that neither he nor father's suspected any more?"

"I think," the doctor gave his opinion with exaggerated deliberation, "it might—in fact, it really will be his best medicine."

She thanked him, stars swimming in her eyes.

www.ingramcontent.com/pod-product-compliance
Lightning Source LLC
Chambersburg PA
CBHW032205190626
46810CB00018B/1650